THE FLIGHT OF THE SHADOW

The Flight
of the
Shadow

George MacDonald

1817

Harper & Row, Publishers, San Francisco

Cambridge, Hagerstown, New York, Philadelphia
London, Mexico City, São Paulo, Sydney

Afterword copyright © 1983 by Harper & Row, Publishers. All rights reserved. Printed in the United States of America. No part of this book may be used or reproduced in any manner whatsoever without written permission except in the case of brief quotations embodied in critical articles and reviews. For information address Harper & Row, Publishers, Inc., 10 East 53rd Street, New York, NY 10022. Published simultaneously in Canada by Fitzhenry & Whiteside, Limited, Toronto.

FIRST EDITION

Designed by Jim Mennick

Library of Congress Cataloging in Publication Data

Macdonald, George, 1824–1905.
   FLIGHT OF THE SHADOW.
   I. Title

PR4967.F5   1983   823'.8   82-48407
ISBN 0-06-250563-7

83 84 85 86 87 10 9 8 7 6 5 4 3 2 1

Contents

CHAPTER 1

Mrs. Day Begins the Story

I AM old, else, I think, I should not have the courage to tell the story I am going to tell. All those concerned in it about whose feelings I am careful, are gone where, thank God, there are no secrets! If they know what I am doing, I know they do not mind. If they were alive to read as I record, they might perhaps now and again look a little paler and wish the leaf turned, but to see the things set down would not make them unhappy: they do not love secrecy. Half the misery in the world comes from trying to look, instead of trying to be, what one is not. I would that not God only but all good men and women might see me through and through. They would not be pleased with everything they saw, but then neither am I, and I would have no coals of fire in my soul's pockets! But my very nature would shudder at the thought of letting one person that loved a secret see into it. Such a one never sees things as they are—would not indeed see what was there, but something shaped and coloured after his own likeness. No one who loves and chooses a secret can be of the pure in heart that shall see God.

Yet how shall I tell even who I am? Which of us is other than a secret to all but God! Which of us can tell, with poorest approximation, what he or she is! Not to touch the mystery of life—that one who is not myself has made me able to say *I,* how little can any of us tell about even those ancestors whose names we know, while yet the nature, and still more the character, of hundreds of them, have shared in determining what *I* means every time one of us utters the word! For myself, I remember neither father nor mother, nor one of their fathers or mothers: how little then can I say as to what I am! But I will tell as much as most of my readers, if ever I have any, will care to know.

I come of a long yeoman-line of the name of Which-cote. In Scotland the Whichcotes would have been called *lairds;* in England they were not called *squires.* Repeatedly had younger sons of it risen to rank and honour, and in several generations would his property have entitled the head of the family to rank as a squire, but at the time when I began to be aware of existence, the family posses-sions had dwindled to one large farm, on which I found myself. Naturally, while some of the family had risen, others had sunk in the social scale; and of the latter was Miss Martha Moon, far more to my life than can appear in my story. I should imagine there are few families in England covering a larger range of social difference than ours. But I begin to think the chief difficulty in writing a book must be to keep out what does not belong to it.

I may mention, however, my conviction that I owe many special delights to the gradual development of my race in certain special relations to the natural ways of the world. That I was myself brought up in such relations appears not enough to account for the intensity of my pleasure in things belonging to simplest life—in everything of the open air, in animals of all kinds, in the economy of field and meadow and moor. I can no more understand my delight in the sweet breath of a cow, than I can explain the process by which, that day in the garden —but I must not forestall, and will say rather—than I can account for the tears which, now I am an old woman, fill my eyes just as they used when I was a child, at sight of the year's first primrose. A harebell, much as I have always loved harebells, never moved me that way! Some will say the cause, whatever it be, lies in my nature, not in my ancestry; that, anyhow, it must have come first to some one—and why not to me? I answer, Everything lies in everyone of us, but has to be brought to the surface. It grows a little in one, more in that one's child, more in that child's child, and so on and on—with curious breaks as of a river which every now and then takes to an underground course. One thing I am sure of—that, however any good thing came, I did not make it; I can only be glad and thankful that in me it came to the surface, to tell me how beautiful must he be who thought of it, and made it in me. Then surely one is nearer, if not to God himself, yet to the things God loves, in the country than amid ugly houses—things that could not have been invented by God, though he made the man that made them. It is not

the fashionable only that love the town and not the country; the men and women who live in dirt and squalor—
their counterparts in this and worse things far more than
they think—are afraid of loneliness, and hate God's
lovely dark.

CHAPTER 2

Miss Martha Moon

LET me look back and see what first things I first remember!

All about my uncle first; but I keep him to the last.
Next, all about Rover, the dog—though for roving, I
hardly remember him away from my side! Alas, he did
not live to come into the story, but I must mention him
here, for I shall not write another book, and, in the
briefest summary of my childhood, to make no allusion
to him would be disloyalty. I almost believe that at one
period, had I been set to say who I was, I should have
included Rover as an essential part of myself. His tail was
my tail; his legs were my legs; his tongue was my tongue!
—so much more did I, as we gambolled together, seem
conscious of his joy than of my own! Surely, among other
and greater mercies, I shall find him again!

The next person I see busy about the place, now here

now there in the house, and seldom outside it, is Miss Martha Moon. The house is large, built at a time when the family was one of consequence, and there was always much to be done in it. The largest room in it is now called the kitchen, but was doubtless called the hall when first it was built. This was Miss Martha Moon's headquarters.

She was my uncle's second cousin, and as he always called her Martha, so did I, without rebuke: every one else about the place called her Miss Martha.

Of much greater worth and much more genuine refinement than tens of thousands the world calls ladies, she never claimed the distinction. Indeed she strongly objected to it. If you had said or implied she was a lady, she would have shrunk as from a covert reflection on the quality of her work. Had she known certain of such as nowadays call themselves lady-helps, I could have understood her objection. I think, however, it came from a stern adherence to the factness—if I may coin the word —of things. She never called a lie a fib.

When she was angry, she always held her tongue; she feared being unfair. She had indeed a rare power of silence. To this day I do not *know,* but am nevertheless sure that, by an instinct of understanding, she saw into my uncle's trouble, and descried, more or less plainly, the secret of it, while yet she never even alluded to the existence of such a trouble. She had a regard for woman's dignity as profound as silent. She was not of those that prate or rave about their rights, forget their duties, and care only for what they count their victories.

She declared herself dead against marriage. One day, while yet hardly more than a child, I said to her thoughtfully,

"I wonder why you hate gentlemen, Martha!"

"Hate 'em! What on earth makes you say such a wicked thing, Orbie?" she answered. "Hate 'em, the poor dears! I love 'em! What did you ever see to make you think I hated your uncle now?"

"Oh! of course! uncle!" I returned; for my uncle was all the world to me. "Nobody could hate uncle!"

"She'd be a bad woman, anyhow, that did!" rejoined Martha. "But did anybody ever hate the person that couldn't do without her, Orbie?"

My name—suggested by my uncle because my mother died at my birth—was a curious one; I believe he made it himself. *Belorba* it was, and it means *Fair Orphan.*

"I don't know, Martha," I replied.

"Well, you watch and see!" she returned. "Do you think I would stay here and work from morning to night if I hadn't some reason for it?—Oh, I like work!" she went on; "I don't deny that. I should be miserable if I didn't work. But I'm not bound to this sort of work. I have money of my own, and I'm no beggar for house-room. But rather than leave your uncle, poor man! I would do the work of a ploughman for him."

"Then why don't you marry him, Martha?" I said, with innocent impertinence.

"Marry him! I wouldn't marry him for ten thousand pounds, child!"

"Why not, if you love him so much? I'm sure he wouldn't mind!"

"Marry him!" repeated Miss Martha, and stood looking at me as if here at last was a creature she could *not* understand; "marry the poor dear man, and make him miserable! I could love any man better than that! Just you open your eyes, my dear, and see what goes on about you. Do you see so many men made happy by their wives? I don't say it's all the wives' fault, poor things! But the fact's the same: there's the poor husbands all the time trying hard to bear it! What with the babies, and the headaches, and the rest of it, that's what it comes to—the husbands are not happy! No, no! A woman can do better for a man than marry him!"

"But mayn't it be the husband's fault—sometimes, Martha?"

"It may; but what better is it for that? What better is the wife for knowing it, or how much happier the husband for not knowing it? As soon as you come to weighing who's in fault, and counting how much, it's all up with the marriage. There's no more comfort in life for either of them! Women are sent into the world to make men happy. I was sent to your uncle, and I'm trying to do my duty. It's nothing to me what other women think; I'm here to serve your uncle. What comes of me, I don't care, so long as I do my work, and don't keep him waiting that made me for it. You may think it a small thing to make a man happy! I don't. God thought him worth making, and he wouldn't be if he was miserable. I've seen one woman make ten men unhappy! I know my calling, Orbie. Nothing would make me marry one of them, poor things!"

"But if they all said as you do, Martha?"

"No doubt the world would come to an end, but it would go out singing, not crying. I don't see that would matter. There would be enough to make each other happy in heaven, and the Lord could make more as they were wanted."

"Uncle says it takes God a long time to make a man!" I ventured to remark.

Miss Martha was silent for a moment. She did not see how my remark bore on the matter in hand, but she had such respect for anything my uncle said, that when she did not grasp it she held her peace.

"Anyhow there's no fear of it for the present!" she answered. "You heard the screed of banns last Sunday!"

I thought you would have a better idea of Miss Martha Moon from hearing her talk, than from any talk about her. To hear one talk is better than to see one. But I would not have you think she often spoke at such length. She was in truth a woman of few words, never troubled or troubling with any verbal catarrh. Especially silent she was when any one she loved was in distress. I have seen her stand moveless for moments, with a look that was the incarnation of essential motherhood—as if her eyes were swallowing up sorrow; as if her soul was ready to be the sacrifice for sin. Then she would turn away with a droop of the eye-lids that seemed to say she saw what it was, but saw also how little she could do for it. Oh the depth of the love-trouble in those eyes of hers!

Martha never set herself to teach me anything, but I could not know Martha without learning something of the genuine human heart. I gathered from her by unconscious assimilation. Possibly, a spiritual action analogous to exosmose and endosmose, takes place between certain souls.

CHAPTER 3

My Uncle

Now I must tell you what my uncle was like.

The first thing that struck you about him would have been, how tall and thin he was. The next thing would have been, how he stooped; and the next, how sad he looked. It scarcely seemed that Martha Moon had been able to do much for him. Yet doubtless she had done, and was doing, more than either he or she knew. He had rather a small head on the top of his long body; and when he stood straight up, which was not very often, it seemed so far away, that someone said he took him for Zacchaeus looking down from the sycamore. *I* never thought of analyzing his appearance, never thought of comparing him with any one else. To me he was the best and most beautiful of men—the first man in all the world. Nor did I change my mind about him ever—I only came to want another to think of him as I did.

His features were in fine proportion, though perhaps too delicate. Perhaps they were a little too small to be properly beautiful. When first I saw a likeness of the poet Shelley, I called out "My uncle!" and immediately began to see differences. He wore a small but long moustache, brushed away from his mouth; and over it his eyes looked large. They were of a clear gray, and very gentle. I know from the testimony of others, that I was right in imagining him a really learned man. That small head of his contained more and better than many a larger head of greater note. He was constantly reading—that is, when not thinking, or giving me the lessons which make me now thank him for half my conscious soul.

Reading or writing or thinking, he made me always welcome to share his room with him; but he seldom took me out walking. He was by no means regular in his habits —regarded neither times nor seasons—went and came like a bird. His hour for going out was unknown to himself, was seldom two days together the same. He would rise up suddenly, even in the middle of a lesson—he always called it "a lesson together"—and without a word walk from the room and the house. I had soon observed that in gloomy weather he went out often, in the sunshine seldom.

The house had a large garden, of a very old-fashioned sort, such a place for the charm of both glory and gloom as I have never seen elsewhere. I have had other eyes opened within me to deeper beauties than I saw in that garden then; my remembrance of it is none the less of an enchanted ground. But my uncle never walked in it. When he walked, it was always out on the moor he went, and what time he would return no one ever knew. His

meals were uninteresting to him—no concern to any one
but Martha, who never uttered a word of impatience, and
seldom a word of anxiety. At whatever hour of the day
he went, it was almost always night when he came home,
often late night. In the house he much preferred his own
room to any other.

  This room, not so large as the kitchen-hall, but quite
as long, it seems to me, when I look back, my earliest
surrounding. It was the centre from which my roving
fancies issued as from their source, and the end of their
journey to which as to their home they returned. It was
a curious place. Were you to see first the inside of the
house and then the outside, you would find yourself at
a loss to conjecture where within it could be situated
such a room. It was not, however, contained in what, to
a cursory glance, passed for the habitable house, and a
stranger would not easily have found the entrance to it.

  Both its nature and situation were in keeping with
certain peculiarities of my uncle's mental being. He was
given to curious inquiries. He would set out to solve now
one now another historical point as odd as uninteresting
to any but a mind capable of starting such a question. To
determine it, he would search book after book, as if it
were a live thing, in whose memory must remain, darkly
stored, thousands of facts, requiring only to be recol-
lected: amongst them might nestle the thing he sought,
and he would dig for it as in a mine that went branching
through the hardened dust of ages. I fancy he read any
old book whatever of English history with the haunting
sense that next moment he might come upon the trace
of certain of his own ancestors of whom he specially
desired to enlarge his knowledge. Whether he started

any new thing in mathematics I cannot tell, but he would sit absorbed, every day and all day long, for weeks, over his slate, suddenly throw it down, walk out for the rest of the day, and leave his calculus, or whatever it was, for months. He read Shakspere as with a microscope, propounding and answering the most curious little questions. It seemed to me sometimes, I confess, that he missed a plain point from his eyes being so sharp that they looked through it without seeing it, having focused themselves beyond it.

A specimen of the kind of question he would ask and answer himself, occurs to me as I write, for he put it to me once as we read together.

"Why," he said, "did Margaret, in *Much ado about Nothing,* try to persuade Hero to wear her other rabato?"

And the answer was,

"Because she feared her mistress would find out that she had been wearing it—namely, the night before, when she personated her."

And here I may put down a remark I heard him make in reference to a theory which itself must seem nothing less than idiotic to any one who knows Shakspere as my uncle knew him. The remark was this—that whoever sought to enhance the fame of lord St. Alban's—he was careful to use the real title—by attributing to him the works of Shakspere, must either be a man of weak intellect, of great ignorance, or of low moral perception; for he cast on the memory of a man already more to be pitied than any, a weight of obloquy such as it were hard to believe anyone capable of deserving. A being with Shakspere's love of human nature, and Bacon's insight into essential truth, guilty of the moral and social atrocities into which his lordship's eagerness after money for scientific research betrayed him, would be a monster as grotesque as abominable.

I record the remark the rather that it shows my uncle could look at things in a large way as well as hunt with a knife-edge. At the same time, devoutly as I honour him, I cannot but count him intended for thinkings of larger scope than such as then seemed characteristic of him. I imagine his early history had affected his faculties, and influenced the mode of their working. How indeed could it have been otherwise!

CHAPTER 4

My Uncle's Room, and My Uncle in It

AT right angles to the long, black and white house, stood a building behind it, of possibly earlier date, but uncertain intent. It had been used for many things before my uncle's time—once as part of a small brewery. My uncle was positive that, whether built for the purpose or not, it had been used as a chapel, and that the house was originally the out-lying cell of some convent. The signs on which he founded this conclusion, I was never able to appreciate: to me, as containing my uncle's study, the wonder-house of my childhood, it was far more interesting than any history could have made it. It had very thick walls, two low stories, and a high roof. Entering it from the court behind the house, every portion of it would seem to an ordinary beholder quite accounted for; but it might have suggested itself to a more comprehending observer, that a considerable space must lie between the roof and the low ceiling of the first floor, which was taken up with the servants' rooms. Of the ground floor, part was used as a dairy, part as a woodhouse, part for certain vegetables, while part stored the turf dug for fuel from the neighbouring moor.

Between this building and the house was a smaller and lower erection, a mere out-house. It also was strongly built, however, and the roof, in perfect condition, seemed newer than the walls: it had been raised and strengthened when used by my uncle to contain a passage leading from the house to the roof of the building just described, in which he was fashioning for himself the retreat which he rightly called his study, for few must be the rooms more continuously thought and read in during one lifetime than this.

I have now to tell how it was reached from the house. You could hardly have found the way to it, even had you set yourself seriously to the task, without having in you a good share of the constructive faculty. The whole was my uncle's contrivance, but might well have been supposed to belong to the troubled times when a good hiding-place would have added to the value of any home.

There was a large recess in the kitchen, of which the hearth, raised a foot or so above the flagged floor, had filled the whole—a huge chimney in fact, built out from the wall. At some later time an oblong space had been cut out of the hearth to a level with the floor, and in it an iron grate constructed for the more convenient burning of coal. Hence the remnant of the raised hearth looked like wide hobs to the grate. The recess as a chimney-corner was thereby spoiled, for coal makes a very different kind of smoke from the aromatic product of wood or peat.

Right and left within the recess, were two common, unpainted doors, with latches. If you opened either, you found an ordinary shallow cupboard, that on the right filled with shelves and crockery, that on the left with brooms and other household implements.

But if, in the frame of the door to the left, you pressed what looked like the head of a large nail, not its door only but the whole cupboard turned inward on unseen hinges, and revealed an ascending stair, which was the approach to my uncle's room. At the head of the stair you went through the wall of the house to the passage under the roof of the out-house, at the end of which a few more steps led up to the door of the study. By that door you entered the roof of the more ancient building. Lighted almost entirely from above, there was no indication outside of the existence of this floor, except one tiny window, with vaguely pointed arch, almost in the very top of the gable. Here lay my nest; this was the bower of my bliss.

Its walls rose but about three feet from the floor ere the slope of the roof began, so that there was a considerable portion of the room in which my tall uncle could not stand upright. There was width enough notwithstanding, in which four as tall as he might have walked abreast up and down a length of at least five and thirty feet.

Not merely the low walls, but the slopes of the roof were filled with books as high as the narrow level portion of the ceiling. On the slopes the bookshelves had of course to be peculiar. My uncle had contrived, and partly himself made them, with the assistance of a carpenter he had known all his life. They were individually fixed to the rafters, each projecting over that beneath it. To get at the highest, he had to stand on a few steps; to reach the lowest, he had to stoop at a right angle. The place was almost a tunnel of books.

By setting a chair on an ancient chest that stood against the gable, and a footstool on the chair, I could mount high enough to get into the deep embrasure of the little window, whence alone to gain a glimpse of the lower world, while from the floor I could see heaven through six skylights, deep framed in books. As far back as I can remember, it was my care to see that the inside of their glass was always bright, so that sun and moon and stars might look in.

The books were mostly in old and dingy bindings, but there were a few to attract the eyes of a child—especially some annuals, in red skil, or embossed leather, or, most bewitching of all, in paper, protected by a tight case of the same, from which, with the help of a ribbon, you drew out the precious little green volume, with its gilt edges and lovely engravings—one of which in particular I remember—a castle in the distance, a wood, a ghastly man at the head of a rearing horse, and a white, mist-like, fleeting ghost, the cause of the consternation. These books had a large share in the witchery of the chamber.

At the end of the room, near the gable-window, but under one of the skylights, was a table of white deal, without cover, at which my uncle generally sat, sometimes writing, oftener leaning over a book. Occasionally, however, he would occupy a large old-fashioned easy chair, under the slope of the roof, in the same end of the room, sitting silent, neither writing nor reading, his eyes fixed straight before him, but plainly upon nothing. They looked as if sights were going out of them rather than coming in at them. When he sat thus, I would sit gazing at him. Oh how I loved him—loved every line of his gentle, troubled countenance! I do not remember the time when I did not know that his face was troubled. It gave the last finishing tenderness to my love for him. It was from no meddlesome curiosity that I sat watching him, from no longing to learn what he was thinking about, or what pictures were going and coming before the eyes of his mind, but from such a longing to comfort him as amounted to pain. I think it was the desire to be near him—in spirit, I mean, for I could be near him in the body any time except when he was out on one of his lonely walks or rides—that made me attend so closely to my studies. He taught me everything, and I yearned to please him, but without this other half-conscious yearning I do not believe I should ever have made the progress he praised. I took indeed a true delight in learning, but I would not so often have shut the book I was enjoying to the full and taken up another, but for the sight or the thought of my uncle's countenance.

I think he never once sat down in the chair I have mentioned without sooner or later rising hurriedly, and going out on one of his solitary rambles.

When we were having our lessons together, as he phrased it, we sat at the table side by side, and he taught me as if we were two children finding out together what it all meant. Those lessons had, I think, the largest share in the charm of the place; yet when, as not unfrequently, my uncle would, in the middle of one of them, rise abruptly and leave me without a word, to go, I knew, far away from the house, I was neither dismayed nor uneasy: I had got used to the thing before I could wonder what it meant. I would just go back to the book I had been reading, or to any other that attracted me: he never required the preparation of any lessons. It was of no use to climb to the window in the hope of catching sight of him, for thence was nothing to be seen immediately below but the tops of high trees and a corner of the yard into which the cow-houses opened, and my uncle was never there. He neither understood nor cared about farming. His elder brother, my father, had been bred to carry on the yeoman-line of the family, and my uncle was trained to the medical profession. My father dying rather suddenly, my uncle, who was abroad at the time, and had not begun to practise, returned to take his place, but never paid practical attention to the farming any more than to his profession. He gave the land in charge to a bailiff, and at once settled down, Martha told me, into what we now saw him. She seemed to imply that grief at my father's death was the cause of his depression, but I soon came to the conclusion that it lasted too long to be so accounted for. Gradually I grew aware—so gradually that at length I seemed to have known it from the first —that the soul of my uncle was harassed with an undying trouble, that some worm lay among the very roots of his life. What change could ever dispel such a sadness as I often saw in that chair! Now and then he would sit there for hours, an open book in his hand perhaps, at which he cast never a glance, all unaware of the eyes of the small maiden fixed upon him, with a whole world of sympathy behind them. I suspect, however, as I believe I have said, that Martha Moon, in her silence, had pierced the heart of the mystery, though she *knew* nothing.

One practical lesson given me now and then in varying form by my uncle, I at length, one day, suddenly and involuntarily associated with the darkness that haunted him. In substance it was this: "Never, my little one, hide anything from those that love you. Never let anything that makes itself a nest in your heart, grow into a secret, for then at once it will begin to eat a hole in it." He would so often say the kind of thing, that I seemed to know when it was coming. But I had heard it as a thing of course, never realizing its truth, and listening to it only because he whom I loved said it.

I see with my mind's eye the fine small head and large eyes so far above me, as we sit beside each other at the deal table. He looked down on me like a bird of prey. His hair—gray, Martha told me, before he was thirty—was tufted out a little, like ruffled feathers, on each side. But the eyes were not those of an eagle; they were a dove's eyes.

"A secret, little one, is a mole that burrows," said my uncle.

The moment of insight was come. A voice seemed suddenly to say within me, "He has a secret; it is biting his heart!" My affection, my devotion, my sacred concern for him, as suddenly swelled to twice their size. It was as if a God were in pain, and I could not help him. I had no desire to learn his secret; I only yearned heart and soul to comfort him. Before long, I had a secret myself for half a day: ever after, I shared so in the trouble of his secret, that I seemed myself to possess or rather to be possessed by one—such a secret that I did not myself know it.

But in truth I had a secret then; for the moment I knew that he had a secret, his secret—the outward fact of its existence, I mean—was my secret. And besides this secret of his, I had then a secret of my own. For I knew that my uncle had a secret, and he did not know that I knew. Therewith came, of course, the question—Ought I to tell him? At once, by the instinct of love, I saw that to tell him would put him in a great difficulty. He might wish me never to let any one else know of it, and how could he say so when he had been constantly warning me to let nothing grow to a secret in my heart? As to telling Martha Moon, much as I loved her, much as I knew she loved my uncle, and sure as I was that anything concerning him was as sacred to her as to me, I dared not commit such a breach of confidence as even to think in her presence that my uncle had a secret. From the hour I had recurrent fits of a morbid terror at the very idea of a secret—as if a secret were in itself a treacherous, poisonous guest, that ate away the life of its host.

But to return, my half-day-secret came in this wise.

CHAPTER 5

My First Secret

I WAS one morning with my uncle in his room. Lessons
were over, and I was reading a marvelous story in one of
my favourite annuals: my uncle had so taught me from
infancy the right handling of books, that he would have
trusted me with the most valuable in his possession. I do
not know how old I was, but that is no matter; man or
woman is aged according to the development of the conscience. Looking up, I saw him stooping over an open
drawer in a cabinet behind the door. I sat on the great
chest under the gable-window, and was away from him
the whole length of the room. He had never told me not
to look at him, had never seemed to object to the presence of my eyes on anything he did, and as a matter of
course I sat observing him, partly because I had never
seen any portion of that cabinet open. He turned to-
wards the sky-light near him, and held up between him

and it a small something, of which I could just see that
it was red, and shone in the light. Then he turned hurriedly, threw it in the drawer, and went straight out,
leaving the drawer open. I knew I had lost his company
for the day.

The moment he was gone, the phantasm of the pretty
thing he had been looking at so intently, came back to
me. Somehow I seemed to understand that I had no right
to know what it was, seeing my uncle had not shown it
me! At the same time I had no law to guide me. He had
never said I was not to look at this or that in the room.
If he had, even if the cabinet had not been mentioned,
I do not think I should have offended; but that does not
make the fault less. For which is the more guilty—the
man who knows there is a law against doing a certain
thing and does it, or the man who feels an authority in
the depth of his nature forbidding the thing, and yet
does it? Surely the latter is greatly the more guilty.

I rose, and went to the cabinet. But when the contents
of the drawer began to show themselves as I drew near,
"I closed my lids, and kept them close," until I had
seated myself on the floor, with my back to the cabinet,
and the drawer projecting over my head like the shelf of
a bracket over its supporting figure. I could touch it with
the top of my head by straightening my back. How long
I sat there motionless, I cannot say, but it seems in retro-
spect at least a week, such a multitude of thinkings went
through my mind. The logical discussion of a thing that
has to be done, a thing awaiting action and not decision
—the experiment, that is, whether the duty or the temptation has the more to say for itself, is one of the straight
roads to the pit. Similarly, there are multitudes who lose

their lives pondering what they ought to believe, while something lies at their door waiting to be done, and rendering it impossible for him who makes it wait, ever to know what to believe. Only a pure heart can understand, and a pure heart is one that sends out ready hands. I knew perfectly well what I ought to do—namely, to shut that drawer with the back of my head, then get up and do something, and forget the shining stone I had seen betwixt my uncle's finger and thumb; yet there I sat debating whether I was not at liberty to do in my uncle's room what he had not told me not to do.

I will not weary my reader with any further description of the evil path by which I arrived at the evil act. To myself it is pain even now to tell that I got on my feet, saw a blaze of shining things, banged-to the drawer, and knew that Eve had eaten the apple. The eyes of my consciousness were opened to the evil in me, through the evil done by me. Evil seemed now a part of myself, so that nevermore should I get rid of it. It may be easy for one regarding it from afar, through the telescope only of a book, to exclaim, "Such a little thing!" but it was I who did it, and not another! it was I, and only I, who could know what I had done, and it was not a little thing! That peep into my uncle's drawer lies in my soul the type of sin. Never have I done anything wrong with such a clear assurance that I was doing wrong, as when I did the thing I had taken most pains to reason out as right.

Like one stunned by an electric shock, I had neither feeling nor care left for anything. I walked to the end of the long room, as far as I could go from the scene of my crime, and sat down on the great chest, with my coffin, the cabinet, facing me in the distance. The first thing, I think, that I grew conscious of, was dreariness. There was nothing interesting anywhere. What should I do? There was nothing to do, nothing to think about, not a book worth reading. Story was suddenly dried up at its fountain. Life was a plain without waterbrooks. If the sky was not "a foul and pestilent congregation of vapours," it was nothing better than a canopy of gray and blue. By degrees my thought settled on what I had done, and in a moment I realized it as it was—a vile thing, and I had lost my life for it! This is the nearest I can come to the expression of what I felt. I was simply in despair. I had done wrong, and the world had closed in upon me; the sky had come down and was crushing me! The lid of my coffin was closed! I should come no more out!

But deliverance came speedily—and in how lovely a way! Into my thought, not into the room, came my uncle! Present to my deepest consciousness, he stood tall, loving, beautiful, sad. I read no rebuke in his countenance, only sorrow that I had sinned, and sympathy with my suffering because of my sin. Then first I knew that I had *wronged* him in looking into his drawer; then first I saw it was his being that made the thing I had done an evil thing. If the drawer had been nobody's, there would have been no wrong in looking into it! And what made it so very bad was that my uncle was so good to me!

With the discovery came a rush of gladsome relief. Strange to say, with the clearer perception of the greatness of the wrong I had done, came the gladness of redemption. It was almost a pure joy to find that it was against my uncle, my own uncle, that I had sinned! That joy was the first gleam through a darkness that had seemed settled on my soul for ever. But a brighter followed; for thus spake the truth within me: "The thing is in your uncle's hands; he is the lord of the wrong you have done; it is to him it makes you a debtor:—he loves you, and will forgive you. Of course he will! He cannot make undone what is done, but he will comfort you, and find some way of setting things right. There must be some way! I cannot be doomed to be a contemptible child to all eternity! It is so easy to go wrong, and so hard to get right! He must help me!"

I sat the rest of the day alone in that solitary room, away from Martha and Rover and everybody. I would that even now in my old age I waited for God as then I waited for my uncle! If only he would come, that I might pour out the story of my fall, for I had sinned after the similitude of Adam's transgression!—only I was worse, for neither serpent nor wife had tempted me!

At tea-time Martha came to find me. I would not go with her. She would bring me my tea, she said. I would not have any tea. With a look like that she sometimes cast on my uncle, she left me. Dear Martha! she had the lovely gift of leaving alone. That evening there was no tea in the house; Martha did not have any.

With the conceit peculiar to repentance and humiliation, I took a curious satisfaction in being hard on myself. I could have taken my meal tolerably well: with the new hope in my uncle as my saviour, came comfort enough for the natural process of getting hungry, and desiring food; but with common, indeed vulgar foolishness, my own righteousness in taking vengeance on my fault was a satisfaction to me. I did not then see the presumption of the sinner's taking vengeance on her own fault, did

not see that I had no right to do that. For how should a
thing defiled punish? With all my great joy in the discovery that the fault was against my uncle, I forgot that
therefore I was in his jurisdiction, that he only had to
deal with it, he alone could punish, as he alone could
forgive it.

It was the end of August, and the night stole swiftly
upon the day. It began to grow very dusk, but I would
not stir. I and the cabinet kept each other dismal company while the gloom deepened into night. Nor did the
night part us, for I and the cabinet filled all the darkness. Had my uncle remained the whole night away, I
believe I should have sat till he came. But, happily both
for my mental suffering and my bodily endurance, he
returned sooner than many a time. I heard the
housedoor open. I knew he would come to the study
before going to his bedroom, and my heart gave a
bound of awe-filled eagerness. I knew also that Martha
never spoke to him when he returned from one of his
late rambles, and that he would not know I was there:
long before she died Martha knew how grateful he was
for her delicate consideration. Martha Moon was not
one of this world's ladies; but there is a country where
the social question is not, "Is she a lady?" but, "How
much of a woman is she?" Martha's name must, I think,
stand well up in the book of life.

My uncle, then, approached his room without knowing
there was a live kernel to the dark that filled it. I hear-
kened to every nearer step as he came up the stair, along
the corridor, and up the short final ascent to the door of
the study. I had crept from my place to the middle of the
room, and, without a thought of consequences, stood

waiting the arrival through the dark, of my deliverer from the dark. I did not know that many a man who would face a battery calmly, will spring a yard aside if a yelping cur dart at him.

My uncle opened the door, and closed it behind him. His lamp and matches stood ready on his table: it was my part to see they were there. With a sigh, which seemed to seek me in the darkness and find me, he came forward through it. I caught him round the legs, and clung to him. He gave a great gasp and a smothered cry, staggered, and nearly fell. "My God!" he murmured.

"Uncle! uncle!" I cried, in greater terror than he; "it's only Orbie! It's only your little one!"

"Oh! it's only my little one, is it?" he rejoined, at once recovering his equanimity, and not for a moment losing the temper so ready, like nervous cat, to spring from most of us when startled.

He caught me up in his arms, and held me to his heart. I could feel it beat against my little person.

"Uncle! uncle!" I cried again. "Don't! Don't!"

"Did I hurt you, my little one?" he said, and relaxing his embrace, held me more gently, but did not set me down.

"No, no!" I answered. "But I've got a secret, and you mustn't kiss me till it is gone. I wish there was a swine to send it into!"

"Give it to me, little one. I will treat it better than a swine would."

"But it mustn't be treated, uncle! It might come again!"

"There is no fear of that, my child! As soon as a secret is told, it is dead. It is a secret no longer."

"Will it be dead, uncle?" I returned. "—But it will be there, all the same, when it is dead—an ugly thing. It will only put off its cloak, and show itself!"

"All secrets are not ugly things when their cloaks are off. The cloak may be the ugly thing, and nothing else."

He stood in the dark, holding me in his arms. But the clouds had cleared off a little, and though there was no moon, I could see the dim blue of the sky-lights, and a little shine from the gray of his hair.

"But mine is an ugly thing," I said, "and I hate it. Please let me put it out of my mouth. Perhaps then it will go dead."

"Out with it, little one."

"Put me down, please," I returned.

He walked to the old chest under the gable-window, seated himself on it, and set me down beside him. I slipped from the chest, and knelt on the floor at his feet, a little way in front of him. I did not touch him, and all was again quite dark about us.

I told him my story from beginning to end, along with a great part of my meditations while hesitating to do the deed. I felt very choky, but forced my way through, talking with a throat that did not seem my own, and sending out a voice I seemed never to have heard before. The moment I ceased, a sound like a sob came out of the darkness. Was it possible my big uncle was crying? Then indeed there was no hope for me! He was horrified at my wickedness, and very sorry to have to give me up! I howled like a wild beast.

"Please, uncle, will you kill me!" I cried, through a riot of sobs that came from me like potatoes from a sack.

"Yes, yes, I will kill you, my darling!" he answered,

"—this way! this way!" and stretching out his arms he found me in the dark, drew me to him, and covered my face with kisses.

"Now," he resumed, "I've killed you alive again, and the ugly secret is dead, and will never come to life any more. And I think, besides, we have killed the hen that lays the egg-secrets!"

He rose with me in his arms, set me down on the chest, lighted his lamp, and carried it to the cabinet. Then he returned, and taking me by the hand, led me to it, opened wide the drawer of offence, lifted me, and held me so that I could see well into it. The light flashed in a hundred glories of colour from a multitude of cut but unset stones that lay loose in it. I soon learned that most of them were of small money-value, but their beauty was none the less entrancing. There were stones of price among them, however, and these were the first he taught me, because they were the most beautiful. My fault had opened a new source of delight: my stone-lesson was now one of the great pleasures of the week. In after years I saw in it the richness of God not content with setting right what is wrong, but making from it a gain: he will not have his children the worse for the wrong they have done! We shall lose nothing by it: he is our father! For the hurting sand-grain, he gives his oyster a pearl.

"There," said my uncle, "you may look at them as often as you please; only mind you put every one back as soon as you have satisfied your eyes with it. You must not put one in your pocket, or carry it about in your hand."

Then he set me down, saying,

"Now you must go to bed, and dream about the pretty

things. I will tell you a lot of stories about them afterward."

We had a way of calling any kind of statement *a story*.

I never cared to ask how it was that, seeing all the same
I had done the wrong thing, the whole weight of it was
gone from me. So utterly was it gone, that I did not even
inquire whether I ought so to let it pass from me. It was
nowhere. In the fire of my uncle's love to me and mine
to him, the thing vanished. It was annihilated. Should I
not be a creature unworthy of life, if, now in my old age,
I, who had such an uncle in my childhood, did not with
my very life believe in God?

I have wondered whether, if my father had lived to
bring me up instead of my uncle, I should have been very
different; but the useless speculation has only driven me
to believe that the relations on the surface of life are but
the symbols of far deeper ties, which may exist without
those correspondent external ones. At the same time,
now that, being old, I naturally think of the coming
change, I feel that, when I see my father, I shall have a
different feeling for him just because he is my father,
although my uncle did all the fatherly toward me. But we
need not trouble ourselves about our hearts, and all their
varying hues and shades of feeling. Truth is at the root
of all existence, therefore everything must come right if
only we are obedient to the truth; and right is the deepest
satisfaction of every creature as well as of God. I wait in
confidence. If things be not as we think, they will both
arouse and satisfy a better *think*, making us glad they are
not as we expected.

CHAPTER 6

I Lose Myself

I HAVE one incident more to relate ere my narrative begins to flow from a quite clear memory.

I was by no means a small bookworm, neither spent all my time in the enchanted ground of my uncle's study. It is true I loved the house, and often felt like a burrowing animal that would rather not leave its hole; but occasionally even at such times would suddenly wake the passion for the open air: I must get into it or die! I was well known in the farmyard, not to the men only, but to the animals also. In the absence of human playfellows, they did much to keep me from selfishness. But far beyond it I took no unfrequent flight—always alone. Neither Martha nor my uncle ever seemed to think I needed looking after; and I am not aware that I should have gained anything by it. I speak for myself; I have no theories about the bringing up of children. I went where and

when I pleased, as little challenged as my uncle himself.
Like him, I took now and then a long ramble over the
moor, fearing nothing, and knowing nothing to fear. I
went sometimes where it seemed as if human foot could
never have trod before, so wild and waste was the prospect, so unknown it somehow looked. The house was
built on the more sloping side of a high hollow just
within the moor, which stretched wide away from the
very edge of the farm. If you climbed the slope, following
a certain rough country road, at the top of it you saw on
the one side the farm, in all the colours and shades of its
outspread, well tilled fields; on the other side, the heath.
If you went another way, through the garden, through
the belt of shrubs and pines that encircled it, and
through the wilderness behind that, you were at once
upon the heath. If then you went as far as the highest
point in sight, wading through the heather, among the
rocks and great stones which in childhood I never
doubted grew also, you saw before you nothing but a
wide, wild level, whose horizon was here and there broken by low hills. But the seeming level was far from flat
or smooth, as I found on the day of the adventure I am
about to relate. I wonder I had never lost myself before.
I suppose then first my legs were able to wander beyond
the ground with which my eyes were familiar.

It had rained all the morning and afternoon. When our
last lesson was over, my uncle went out, and I betook
myself to the barn, where I amused myself in the straw.
By this time Rover must have gone back to his maker, for
I remember as with me a large, respectable dog of the
old-fashioned mastiff-type, who endured me with a pa-
tience that amounted almost to friendliness, but never

followed me about. When I grew hungry, I went into the house to have my afternoon-meal. It was called tea, but I knew nothing about tea, while in milk I was a connoisseur. I could tell perfectly to which of the cows I was indebted for the milk I happened at any time to be drinking: Miss Martha never allowed the milks of the different cows to be mingled.

Just as my meal was over, the sun shone with sudden brilliance into my very eyes. The storm was breaking up, and vanishing in the west. I threw down my spoon, and ran, hatless as usual, from the house. The sun was on the edge of the hollow; I made straight for him. The bracken was so wet that my legs almost seemed walking through a brook, and my body through a thick rain. In a moment I was sopping; but to be wet was of no consequence to me. Not for many years was I able to believe that damp could hurt.

When I reached the top, the sun was yet some distance above the horizon, and I had gone a good way toward him before he went down. As he sank he sent up a wind, which blew a sense of coming dark. The wind of the sunset brings me, ever since, a foreboding of tears: it seems to say—"Your day is done; the hour of your darkness is at hand." It grew cold, and a feeling of threat filled the air. All about the grave of the buried sun, the clouds were angry with dusky yellow and splashes of gold. They lowered tumulous and menacing. Then, lo! they had lost courage; their bulk melted off in fierce vapour, gold and gray, and the sharp outcry of their shape was gone. As I recall the airy scene, that horizon looks like the void between a cataclysm and the moving afresh of the spirit of God upon the face of the waters.

I went on and on, I do not know why. Something enticed me, or I was plunged in some meditation, then absorbing, now forgotten, not necessarily worthless. I am jealous of moods that can be forgotten, but such may leave traces in the character. I wandered on. What ups and downs there were! how uneven was the surface of the moor! The feet learned what the eyes had not seen.

All at once I woke to the fact that mountains hemmed me in. They looked mountains, though they were but hills. What had become of home? where was it? The light lingering in the west might surely have shown me the direction of it, but I remember no west—nothing but a deep hollow and dark hills. I was lost!

I was not exactly frightened at first. I knew no cause of dread. I had never seen a tramp even; I had no sense of the inimical. I knew nothing of the danger from cold and exposure. But awe of the fading light and coming darkness awoke in me. I began to be frightened, and fear is like other live things: once started, it grows. Then first I thought with dismay, which became terror, of the slimy bogs and the deep pools in them. But just as my heart was dying within me, I looked to the hills—with no hope that from them would come my aid—and there, on the edge of the sky, lifted against it, in a dip between two of the hills, was the form of a lady on horseback. I could see the skirt of her habit flying out against the clouds as she rode. Had she been a few feet lower, so as to come between me and the side of the hill instead of the sky, I should not have seen her; neither should I if she had been a few hundred yards further off. I shrieked at the thought that she did not see me, and I could not make her hear me. She started, turned, seemed to look whence the cry could have come, but kept on her way. Then I shrieked in earnest, and began to run wildly toward her. I think she saw me—that my quicker change of place detached my shape sufficiently to make it discernible. She pulled up, and sat like a statue, waiting me. I kept on calling as I ran, to assure her I was doing my utmost, for I feared she might grow impatient and leave me. But at last it was slowly indeed I staggered up to her, spent. My foot caught, and as I fell, I clasped the leg of her horse: I had no fear of animals more than of human beings. He was startled, and rearing drew his leg from my arms. But he took care not to come down on me. I rose to my feet, and stood panting.

What the lady said, or what I answered, I cannot recall. The next thing I remember is stumbling along by her side, for she made her horse walk that I might keep up with her. She talked a little, but I do not remember what she said. It is all a dream now, a far-off one. It must have been like a dream at the time, I was so exhausted. I remember a voice descending now and then, as if from the clouds—a cold musical voice, with something in it that made me not want to hear it. I remember her saying that we were near her house, and would soon be there. I think she had found out from me where I lived.

All the time I never saw her face: it was too dark. I do not think she once spoke kindly to me. She said I had no business to be out alone; she wondered at my father and mother. I think I was too tired to tell her I had no father or mother. When I did speak, she indicated neither by sound nor movement that she heard or heeded what I said. She sat up above me in the dark, unpleasant, and all but unseen—a riddle which the troubled child stum-

bling along by her horse's side did not want solved. Had
there been anything to call light, I should have run away
from her. Vague doubts of witches and ogresses crossed
my mind, but I said to myself the stories about them were
not true, and kept on as best I could.

Before we reached the house, we had left the heath,
and were moving along lanes. The horse seemed to walk
with more confidence, and it was harder for me to keep
up with him. I was so tired that I could not feel my legs.
I stumbled often, and once the horse trod on my foot. I
fell; he went on; I had to run limping after him. At last
we stopped. I could see nothing. The lady gave a musical
cry. A voice and footsteps made answer; and presently
came the sound of a gate on its hinges. A long dark piece
of road followed. I knew we were among trees, for I
heard the wind in them over our heads. Then I saw lights
in windows, and presently we stopped at the door of a
great house. I remember nothing more of that night.

CHAPTER 7

The Mirror

I woke the next morning in a strange bed, and for a long time could not think how I came to be there. A maid appeared, and told me it was time to get up. Greatly to my dislike, she would insist on dressing me. My clothes looked very miserable, I remember, in consequence of what they had gone through the night before. She was kind to me, and asked me a great many questions, but paid no heed to my answers—a treatment to which I had not been used: I think she must have been the lady's maid. When I was ready, she took me to the housekeeper's room, where I had bread and milk for breakfast. Several servants, men and women, came and went, and I thought they all looked at me strangely. I concluded they had no little girls in that house. Assuredly there was small favour for children in it. In some houses the child is as a stranger; in others he rules:

neither such house is in the kingdom of heaven. I must have looked a forlorn creature as I sat, or perched rather, on the old horsehair-sofa in that dingy room. Nobody said more than a word or so to me. I wondered what was going to be done with me, but I had long been able to wait for what would come. At length, after, as it seemed, hours of weary waiting, during which my heart grew sick with longing after my uncle, I was, without a word of explanation, led through long passages into a room which appeared enormous. There I was again left a long while—this time alone. It was all white and gold, and had its walls nearly covered with great mirrors from floor to ceiling, which, while it was indeed of great size, was the cause of its looking so immeasurably large. But it was some time before I discovered this, for I was not accustomed to mirrors. Except the small one on my little dressing-table, and one still less on Martha's, I had scarcely seen a mirror, and was not prepared for those sheets of glass in narrow gold frames.

I went about, looking at one thing and another, but handling nothing: my late secret had cured me of that. Weary at last, I dropped upon a low chair, and would probably have soon fallen asleep, had not the door opened, and some one come in. I could not see the door without turning, and was too tired and sleepy to move. I sat still, staring, hardly conscious, into the mirror in front of me. All at once I descried in it my uncle—but only to see him grow white as death, and turn away, reeling as if he would fall. The sight so bewildered me that, instead of rushing to embrace him, I sat frozen. He clapped his hands to his eyes, steadied himself, stood for a moment rigid, then came straight toward me. But, to my added astonishment, he gave me no greeting, or showed any sign of joy at having found me. Never before had he seen me for the first time any day, without giving me a kiss; never before, it seemed to me, had he spoken to me without a smile: I had been lost and was found, and he was not glad! The strange reception fell on me like a numbing spell. I had nothing to say, no impulse to move, no part in the present world. He caught me up in his arms, hid his face upon me, knocked his shoulder heavily against the door-post as he went from the room, walked straight through the hall, and out of the house. I think no one saw us as we went; I am sure neither of us saw any one. With long strides he walked down the avenue, never turning his head. Not until we were on the moor, out of sight of the house, did he stop. Then he set me down; and then first we discovered that he had left his hat behind. For all his carrying of me, and going so fast —and I must have been rather heavy—his face had no colour in it.

"Shall I run and get it, uncle?" I said, as I saw him raise his hand to his head, and find no hat there to be taken off. "I should be back in a minute!"

It was the first word spoken between us.

"No, my little one," he answered, wiping his forehead: his voice sounded far away, like that of one speaking in a dream; "I can't let you out of my sight. I've been wandering the moor all night looking for you!"

With that he caught me up again, and pressing his face to mine, walked with me thus, for a long quarter of a mile, I should think. Oh how safe I felt!—and how

happy!—happy beyond smiling! I loved him before, but
I never knew before what it was to lose him and find him
again.

"Tell me," he said at length.

I told him all, and he did not speak a word until my tale
was finished.

"Were you very frightened," he then asked, "when
you found you had lost your way, and darkness was coming?"

"I was frightened, or I would not have gone to the
lady. But I wish I had staid on the moor for you to find
me. I knew you would soon be out looking for me. Until
she came I comforted myself with thinking that perhaps
even then you were on the moor, and I might see you any
moment."

"What else did you think of?"

"I thought that God was out on the moor, and if you
were not there, he would keep me company."

"Ah!" said my uncle, as if thinking to himself; "she but
needs him the more when I am with her!"

"Yes, of course!" I answered; "I need him then for you
as well as for myself."

"That is very true, my child!—Shall I tell you one thing
I thought of while looking for you?"

"Please, uncle."

"I thought how Jesus' father and mother must have
felt when they were looking for him."

"And they needn't have been so unhappy if they had
thought who he was—need they?"

"Certainly not. And I needn't have been so unhappy
if I had thought who you were. But I was terribly frightened, and there I was wrong."

"Who am I, uncle?"

"Another little one of the same father as he."

"Why were you frightened, uncle?"

"I was afraid of your being frightened."

"I hardly had time to be frightened before the lady came."

"Yes; you see I needn't have been so unhappy!"

My uncle always treated me as if I could understand him perfectly. This came, I see now, from the essential childlikeness of his nature, and from no educational theory.

"Sometimes," he went on, "I look all around me to see if Jesus is out anywhere, but I have never seen him yet!"

"We shall see him one day, sha'n't we?" I said, craning round to look into his eyes, which were my earthly paradise. Nor are they a whit less dear to me, nay, they are dearer, that he has been in God's somewhere, that is, the heavenly paradise, for many a year.

"I think so," he answered, with a sigh that seemed to swell like a sea-wave against me, as I sat on his arm; "—I hope so. I live but for that—and for one thing more."

There are some, I fancy, who would blame him for not being sure, and bring text after text to prove that he ought to have been sure. But oh those text-people! They look to me, not like the clay-sparrows that Jesus made fly, but like bird-skins in a glass-case, stuffed with texts. The doubt of a man like my uncle must be a far better thing than their assurance!

"Would you have been frightened if you had met him on the moor last night, little one?" he asked, after a pause.

"Oh, no, uncle!" I returned. "I should have thought it was you till I came nearer, and then I should have known who it was! He wouldn't like a big girl like me to be frightened at him—would he?"

"Indeed not!" answered my uncle fervently; but again his words brought with them a great sigh, and he said no more.

When we reached home, he gave me up to Martha, and went out again—nor returned before I was in bed. But he came to my room, and waked me with a kiss, which sent me faster asleep than before.

CHAPTER 8

Thanatos and Zoe

I THINK it must have been soon after this that my uncle bought himself a horse. I know something of horses now —that is, if much riding and much love suffice to give a knowledge of them—and the horse which was a glory and a wonder to me then, is a glory and a wonder to me still. He was large, big-boned, and powerful, with less beauty but more grandeur than a thoroughbred, and full of a fiery gentleness. He was the very horse for sir Philip Sidney!

One day, after he had had him for several months, and had let no one saddle him but himself, therefore knew him perfectly, and knew that the horse knew his master, I happened to be in the yard as he mounted. The moment he was in the saddle, he bent down to me, and held out his hand.

"Come with me, little one," he said.

Almost ere I knew, I was in the saddle before him. I grasped his hand, instinctively caught with my foot at his, and was astride the pommel. I will not say I sat very comfortably, but the memory of that day's delight will never leave me—not "through all the secular to be." There must be a God to the world tht could give any such delight as fell then to the share of one little girl! I think my uncle must soon after have got another sad- dle, for I have no recollection of any more discomfort; I remember only the delight of the motion of the horse under me.

For, after this, I rode with him often, and he taught me to ride as surely not many have been taught. When he saw me so at home in my seat as to require no support, he made me change my position, and go behind him. There I sat sideways on a cloth, like a lady of old time on a pillion. When I had got used to this, my uncle made me stand on the horse's broad back, holding on by his shoul- ders; and it was wonderful how soon, and how uncon- sciously, I accommodated myself to every motion of the strength that bore me, learning to keep my place by pure balance like a rope-dancer. I had soon quite forgotten to hold by my uncle, and without the least support rode as comfortably, and with as much confidence, as any rider in a circus, though with a far less easy pace under me. When my uncle found me capable of this, he was much pleased, though a little nervous at times.

Able now to ride his big horse any way, he brought me one afternoon the loveliest of Shetland ponies, not very small. With the ordinary human distrust in good, I could hardly believe she was meant for me. She was a dappled gray—like the twilight of a morning after rain, my uncle said. He called her Zoe, which means Life. His own horse he called Thanatos, which means Death. Such as understood it, thought it a terrible name to give a horse. For most people are so afraid of Death that they regard his very name with awe.

My uncle had a riding-habit made for me, and after a week found I could give him no more trouble with my horsewomanship. At once I was at home on my new friend's back, with vistas of delight innumerable opening around me, and from that day my uncle seldom rode without me. When he went wandering, it was almost always on foot, and then, as before, he was always alone. The idea of offering to accompany him on such an occasion, had never occurred to me.

But one stormy autumn afternoon—most of my memories seem of the autumn—my uncle looked worse than usual when he went out, and I felt, I think for the first time, a vague uneasiness about him. Perhaps I had been thinking of him more; perhaps I had begun to wonder what the secret could be that made him so often seem unhappy. Anyhow this evening the desire awoke to be with him in his trouble whatever it was. There was no curiosity in the feeling, I think, only the desire to serve him as I had never served him yet. I had been, as long as I could remember, always at his beck or lightest call; now I wanted to come when needed without being called. Was it impossible a girl should do anything for a man in his trouble? He, a great man, had helped a little girl out of the deepest despair; could the little girl do nothing for the great man? That the big people should do everything, did not seem fair! He had told me once that the world was held together by what every one could do that the others could not do: there must be something I could do that he could not do!

The rain was coming down on the roof like the steady tramp of distant squadrons. I was in the study, therefore near the tiles, and that was how the rain always sounded upon them. Tramp, tramp, tramp, came the whole army of things, riding, riding, to befall my uncle and me. Tramp, tramp, came the troops of the future, to take the citadel of the present! I was not afraid of them, neither sought to imagine myself afraid! I had no picture in my mind of any evil that could assail me. A little grove of black poplars under the gable-window, kept swaying their expostulations, and moaning their entreaties. The great rushing blasts of the wind through their rooted resistance, made the music of the band that accompanied the march of the unknown. I sat and listened, with the vague conviction that something was being done somewhere. It could not be that only the wind and the trees and the rain were in all that wailing and marching! The Powers of life and death must somewhere be at work! Then rose before me the face of my uncle, as he walked from the room, haloed in a sorrowful stillness. If only I could be with him! If only I knew where to seek him! Wishing, wishing, I sat and listened to the rain and the wind.

Suddenly I found myself on my feet, making for the door. I would not have ventured alone upon the moor in such a night, but I should have Zoe with me, who knew all the ways of it—had doubtless been used to bogs in her own country, and her mother before her! Like a small elephant, she would put out her little foot, and tap, and sound, to see if the surface would bear her—if the questionable spot was what it looked to her mistress, or what she herself doubted it. When she had once made up her mind in the negative, no foolish attempt of mine could overpersuade her—could make her trust our weight on it a hair's-breadth. In a bog the greenest spots are the most dangerous, and Zoe knew it: the matted roots might be afloat on a fathomless depth of water. Backed by my uncle, she soon taught me to be as much afraid of those green spots as she was herself. I had learned to trust her thoroughly.

I took my way to the stable, with a hug and a kiss to Martha as I passed her in the kitchen. I got the cowboy to saddle Zoe, fearing I might not persuade one of the big men on such a night, and I was not quite able myself to tighten the girths properly. She had not been out all day, and when I mounted, she danced at the prospect of a gallop.

I took with me the little lantern I went about the place with when there was no moon, and with this alight in my hand, we darted off at a tight-reined gallop into the wet blowing night. What I was going for I did not know, beyond being with my uncle. So far was I from any fear, that, but for my shadowy uneasiness about him, I should have been filled full of the wild joy of battle with the elements. The first part of the way, I had to cling to the saddle: not otherwise could I keep my seat against the wind, which blew so fiercely on me sideways, that it threatened to blow me out of it.

I had not gone far before the saddle began to turn round with me; I was slipping to the ground. I pulled up, dismounted, undid the girths with difficulty, set the saddle straight, then pulled at every strap with all my might.

It was to no purpose: I could not get another hole out of one of them. I mounted and set off again; but the moment a stronger blast came, the saddle began to turn. Then I thought of something to try: dismounting once more, I got up on the off side. The wind now pushed me on to the saddle, freeing it from my leverage, while I had, besides, the use of my legs against the wind, so that we got on bravely, my Zoe and I. But, alas! my lantern was out, and it was impossible to light it again, so that I had now no arrow to shoot at random for my uncle's eye. Before long we reached a tolerable cart-track, which led across the waste to a village, and the wind being now behind us, I resumed the more comfortable seat in the saddle.

We were going at a good speed, and had ridden, as I judged, about three miles, when there came a great flash of lightning—not like any flash I had ever seen before. It was neither the reflection of lightning below the horizon, nor the sudden zigzagged blade, the very idea of force without weight; it was the burst of a ball-headed torrent of fire from a dark cloud, like water sudden from a mountain's heart, which went rushing down a rugged channel, as if the cloud were indeed a mountain, and the fire one of its cataracts. Its endurance was momentary, but its moments might have been counted, for it lasted appreciably longer than an ordinary flash, revealing to my eyes what remains on my mind clear as the picture of some neighbouring tree on the skin of one slain by lightning. The torrent tumbled down the cloud and vanished, but left with me the vision of a man, plainly my uncle, a few hundred yards from me, on a gigantic gray horse, which reared high with fright. But for its size I could have testified before a magistrate, that I had not only seen that horse in the stable as my pony was being saddled, but had stroked and kissed him on the nose. I conceived at once that his apparent size was an illusion caused by the suddenness and keenness of the light, and that my uncle had come home before I had well reached the moor, and had ridden out after me. With a wild cry of delight, I turned at once to leave the road and join him. But the thunder that moment burst with a terrific bellow, and swallowed my cry. The same instant, however, came through it from the other side the voice of my uncle only a few yards away.

"Stay, little one," he shouted; "stay where you are. I will be with you in a moment."

I obeyed, as ever and always without a thought I obeyed the slightest word of my uncle: Zoe and I stood as if never yet parted from chaos and the dark, for Zoe too loved his voice. The wind rose suddenly from a lull to a great roar, emptying a huge cloudful of rain upon us, so that I heard no sound of my uncle's approach; but presently out of the dark an arm was around me, and my head was lying on my uncle's bosom. Then the dark and the rain seemed the natural elements for love and confidence.

"But, uncle," I murmured, full of wonder which had had no time to take shape, "how is it?"

He answered in a whisper that seemed to dread the ear of the wind, lest it should hear him—

"You saw, did you?"

"I saw you upon Death away there in the middle of the lightning. I was going to you. I don't know what to think."

My uncle and I often called the horse by his English name.

"Neither do I," he returned, with a strange half-voice, as if he were choking. "It must have been—I don't know what. There is a deep bog away just there. It must be a lake by now!"

"Yes, uncle; I might have remembered! but how was I to think of that when I saw you there—on dear old Death too! He's the last of horses to get into a bog: he knows his own weight too well!"

"But why did you come out on such a night? What possessed you, little one—in such a storm? I begin to be afraid what next you may do."

"I never do anything—now—that I think you would mind me doing," I answered. "But if you will write out a little book of *mays* and *maynots*, I will learn it by heart."

"No, no," he returned; "we are not going back to the tables of the law! You have a better law written in your heart, my child; I will trust to that.—But tell me why you came out on such a night—and as dark as pitch."

"Just because it was such a night, uncle, and you were out in it," I answered. "Ain't I your own little girl? I hope you ain't sorry I came, uncle! I am glad; and I shouldn't like ever to be glad at what made you sorry."

"What are you glad of?"

"That I came—because I've found you. I came to look for you."

"Why did you come to-night more than any other night?"

"Because I wanted so much to see you. I thought I might be of use to you."

"You are always of use to me; but why did you think of it just to-night?"

"I don't know.—I am older than I was last night," I replied.

He seemed to understand me, and asked me no more questions.

All the time, we had been standing still in the storm. He took Zoe's head and turned it toward home. The dear creature set out with slow leisurely step, heedless apparently of storm and stable. She knew who was by her side, and he must set the pace!

As we went my uncle seemed lost in thought—and no wonder! for how could the sight we had seen be accounted for! Or what might it indicate?

Many were the strange tales I had read, and my conviction was that the vision belonged to the inexplicable. It grew upon me that I had seen my uncle's double. That he should see his own double would not in itself have much surprised me—or, indeed, that I should see it; but I had never read of another person seeing a double at the same time with the person doubled. During the next few days I sought hard for some possible explanation of what had occurred, but could find nothing parallel to it within the scope of my knowledge. I tried *fata morgana, mirage, parhelion,* and whatever I had learned of recognized illusion, but in vain sought satisfaction, or anything pointing in the direction of satisfaction. I was compelled to leave the thing alone. My uncle kept silence about it, but seemed to brood more than usual. I think he too was convinced that it must have another explanation than present science would afford him. Once I ventured to ask if he had come to any conclusion; with a sad smile, he answered,

"I am waiting, little one. There is much we have to wait for. Where would be the good of having your mind made up wrong? It only stands in the way of getting it made up right!"

By degrees the thing went into the distance, and I ceased even speculating upon it. But one little fact I may mention ere I leave it—that, just as I was reaching a state of quiet mental prorogation, I suddenly remembered that, the moment after the flash, my Zoe, startled as she was, gave out a low whinny; I remembered the quiver of it under me: she too must have seen her master's double!

CHAPTER 9

The Garden

I REMEMBER nothing more to disturb the even flow of my life till I was nearly seventeen. Many pleasant things had come and gone; many pleasant things kept coming and going. I had studied tolerably well—at least my uncle showed himself pleased with the progress I had made and was making. I know even yet a good deal more than would be required for one of these modern degrees feminine. I had besides read more of the older literature of my country than any one I have met except my uncle. I had also this advantage over most students, that my knowledge was gained without the slightest prick of the spur of emulation—purely in following the same delight in myself that shone radiant in the eyes of my uncle as he read with me. I had this advantage also over many, that, perhaps from impression of the higher mind, I saw and learned a thing not merely as a fact whose glory lay in the mystery of its undeveloped harmonics, but as the harbinger of an unknown advent. For as long as I can remember, my heart was given to expectation, was tuned to long waiting. I constantly felt—felt without thinking—that something was coming. I feel it now. Were I young I dared not say so. How could I, compassed about with so great a cloud of witnesses to the common-place! Do I not see their superior smile, as, with voices sweetly acidulous, they quote in reply—

> Love is well on the way;
> He'll be here to-day,
>   Or, at latest, the end of the week;
> Too soon you will find him,
> And the sorrow behind him
>   You will not go out to seek!

Would they not tell me that such expectation was but the shadow of the cloud called love, hanging no bigger than a man's hand on the far horizon, but fraught with storm for mind and soul, which, when it withdrew, would carry with it the glow and the glory and the hope of life; being at best but the mirage of an unattainable paradise, therefore direst of deceptions! Little do such suspect that their own behaviour has withered their faith, and their unbelief dried up their life. They can now no more believe in what they once felt, than a cloud can believe in the rainbow it once bore on its bosom. But I am old, therefore dare to say that I expect more and better and higher and lovelier things than I have ever had. I am not going home to God to say—"Father, I have imagined more beautiful things than thou art able to make true! They were so good that thou thyself art either not good enough to will them, or not strong enough to make them. Thou couldst but make thy creature dream of them, because thou canst but dream of them thyself." Nay, nay! In the faith of him to whom the Father shows all things he does, I expect lovelier gifts than I ever have been, ever shall be able to dream of asleep, or imagine awake.

I was now approaching the verge of womanhood. What lay beyond it I could ill descry, though surely a vague power of undeveloped prophecy dwells in every created thing—even in the bird ere he chips his shell.

Should I dare, or could I endure to write of what lies now to my hand, if I did not believe that not our worst but our best moments, not our low but our lofty moods, not our times logical and scientific, but our times instinctive and imaginative, are those in which we perceive the truth! In them we behold it with a beholding which is one with believing. And,

> Though nothing can bring back the hour
> Of splendour in the grass, of glory in the flower,

could not Wordsworth, and cannot we, call up the vision of that hour? and has not its memory almost, or even altogether, the potency of its presence? Is not the very thought of any certain flower enough to make me believe in that flower—believe it to mean all it ever seemed to mean? That *these* eyes may never more rest upon it with the old delight, means little, and matters nothing. I have other eyes, and shall have yet others. If I thought, as so many have degraded themselves to think, that the glory of things in the morning of love was a glamour cast upon the world, no outshine of indwelling radiance, should I care to breathe one day more the air of this or of any world? Nay, nay, but there dwells in everything the Father hath made, the fire of the burning bush, as at home in his son dwelt the glory that, set free, broke out from him on the mount of his transfiguration. The happy-making vision of things that floods the gaze of the youth, when first he lives in the marvel of loving, and being loved by, a woman, is the true vision—and the more likely to be the true one, that, when he gives way to selfishness, he loses faith in the vision, and sinks back into the commonplace unfaith of the beggarly world—a disappointed, sneering worshipper of power and money —with this remnant of the light yet in him, that he grumbles at the gloom its departure has left behind. He confesses by his soreness that the illusion ought to have been true; he seldom confesses that he loved himself more than the woman, and so lost her. He lays the blame on God, on the woman, on the soullessness of the universe—anywhere but on the one being in which he is interested enough to be sure it exists—his own precious, greedy, vulgar self. Would I dare to write of love, if I did not believe it a true, that is, an eternal thing!

It was a summer of exceptional splendour in which my eyes were opened to "the glory of the sum of things." It was not so hot of the sun as summers I have known, but there were so many gentle and loving winds about, with never point or knife-edge in them, that it seemed all the housework of the universe was being done by ladies. Then the way the odours went and came on those sweet winds! and the way the twilight fell asleep into the dark! and the way the sun rushed up in the morning, as if he cried, like a boy, "Here I am! The Father has sent me!

Isn't it jolly!" I saw more sun-rises that year than any year before or since. And the grass was so thick and soft! There must be grass in heaven! And the roses, both wild and tame, that grew together in the wilderness!—I think you would like to hear about the wilderness.

When I grew to notice, and think, and put things together, I began to wonder how the wilderness came there. I could understand that the solemn garden, with its great yew-hedges and alleys, and its oddly cut box-trees, was a survival of the stately old gardens haunted by ruffs and farthingales; but the wilderness looked so much younger that I was perplexed with it, especially as I saw nothing like it anywhere else. I asked my uncle about it, and he explained that it was indeed after an old fashion, but that he had himself made the wilderness, mostly with his own hands, when he was young. This surprised me, for I had never seen him touch a spade, and hardly ever saw him in the garden: when I did, I always felt as if something was going to happen. He said he had in it tried to copy the wilderness laid out by lord St. Alban's in his essays. I found the volume, and soon came upon the essay, On Gardens. The passage concerning the wilderness, gave me, and still gives me so much delight, that I will transplant it like a rose-bush into this wilderness of mine, hoping it will give like pleasure to my reader.

"For the heath, which was the third part of our plot, I wish it to be framed, as much as may be, to a naturall wildnesse. Trees I would have none in it; but some thickets, made onely of sweetbriar, and honnysuckle, and some wild vine amongst; and the ground set with violets, strawberries, and primeroses. For these are sweete, and prosper in the shade. And these to be in the heath, here and there not in any order. I like also little heapes, in the nature of mole-hils (such as are in wilde heaths) to be set, some with wilde thyme; some with pincks; some with germander, that gives a good flower to the eye; some with periwinckle; some with violets; some with strawber- ries; some with couslips; some with daisies; some with red roses; some with lilium convallium; some with sweet- williams red; some with beares-foot; and the like low flowers, being withall sweet and sightly. Part of which heapes, to be with standards, of little bushes, prickt upon their top, and part without. The standards to be roses; juniper; holly; beareberries (but here and there, because of the smell of their blossome;) red currans; gooseber- ries; rosemary; bayes; sweetbriar; and such like. But these standards, to be kept with cutting, that they grow not out of course."

Just such, in all but the gooseberries and currants, was the wilderness of our garden: you came on it by a sudden labyrinthine twist at the end of a narrow alley of yew, and a sudden door in the high wall. My uncle said he liked well to see roses in the kitchen-garden, but not goose- berries in the flower-garden, especially a wild flower- garden. Wherein lies the difference, I never quite made out, but I feel a difference. My main delight in the wilder- ness was to see the roses among the heather—particu- larly the wild roses. When I was grown up, the wilderness always affected me like one of Blake's, or one of Beddoes's yet wilder lyrics. To make it, my uncle had taken in a part of the heath, which came close up to the garden, leaving plenty of the heather and ling. The pro- tecting fence enclosed a good bit of the heath just as it was, so that the wilderness melted away into the heath, and into the wide moor—the fence, though contrived so as to be difficult to cross, being so low that one had to look for it.

Everywhere the inner garden was surrounded with brick walls, and hedges of yew within them; but immediately behind the house, the wall to the lane was not very high.

CHAPTER 10

Once More a Secret

ONE day in June I had gone into the garden about one o'clock, whether with or without object I forget. I had just seen my uncle start for Wittenage. Hearing a horse's hoofs in the lane that ran along the outside of the wall, I looked up. The same moment the horse stopped, and the face of his rider appeared over the wall, between two stems of yew, and two great flowers of purple lilac, in shape like two perfect bunches of swarming bees. It was the face of a youth of eighteen, and beautiful with a right manly beauty.

The moment I looked on this face, I fell into a sort of trance—that is, I entered for a moment some condition of existence beyond the ramparts of what commonly we call life. Love at first sight it was that initiated the strange experience. But understand me: real as what immediately followed was to the consciousness, there was no actual fact in it.

I stood gazing. My eyes seemed drawn, and drawing my person toward the vision. Isolate over the garden-wall was the face; the rest of the man and all the horse were hidden behind it. Betwixt the yew stems and the two great lilac flowers—how heart and brain are yet filled with the old scent of them!—my face, my mouth, my lips met his. I grew blind as with all my heart I kissed him. Then came a flash of icy terror, and a shudder which it frights me even now to recall. Instantly I knew that but a moment had passed, and that I had not moved an inch from the spot where first my eyes met his.

But my eyes yet rested on his; I could not draw them away. I could not free myself. Helplessness was growing agony. His voice broke the spell. He lifted his hunting-cap, and begged me to tell him the way to the next village. My self-possession returned, and the joy of its restoration drove from me any lingering embarrassment. I went forward, and without a faltering tone, I believe, gave him detailed directions. He told me afterwards that, himself in a state of bewildered surprise, he thought me the coolest young person he had ever had the fortune to meet. Why should one be pleased to know that she looked quite different from what she felt? There is something wrong there, surely! I acknowledge the something wrong, but do not understand it. He lifted his cap again, and rode away.

I stood still at the foot of the lilac-tree, and, from a vapour, condensed, not to a stone, but to a world, in which a new Flora was about to be developed. If no new spiritual sense was awakened in me, at least I was aware of a new consciousness. I had never been to myself what I was now.

Terror again seized me: the face might once more look

over the wall, and find me where it had left me! I turned, and went slowly away from the house, gravitating to the darkest part of the garden.

"What has come to me," I said, "that I seek the darkness? Is this another secret? Am I in the grasp of a new enemy?"

And with that came the whirlwind of perplexity. Must I go the first moment I knew I could find him, and tell my uncle what had happened, and how I felt? or must I have, and hold, and cherish in silent heart, a thing so wondrous, so precious, so absorbing? Had I not deliberately promised—of my own will and at my own instance —never again to have a secret from him? Was this a secret? Was it not a secret?

The storm was up, and went on. The wonder is that, in the fire of the new torment, I did not come to loathe the very thought of the young man—which would have delivered me, if not from the necessity of confession, yet from the main difficulty in confessing.

I said to myself that the old secret was of a wrong done to my uncle; that what had made me miserable then was a bad secret. The perception of this difference gave me comfort for a time, but not for long. The fact remained, that I knew something concerning myself which my best friend did not know. It was, and I could not prevent it from being, a barrier between us!

Yet what was it I was concealing from him? What had I to tell him? How was I to represent a thing of which I knew neither the name nor the nature, a thing I could not describe? Could I confess what I did not understand? The thing might be what, in the tales I had read, was called love, but I did not know that it was. It might be something new, peculiar to myself; something for which there was no word in the language! How was I to tell? I saw plainly that, if I tried to convey my new experience, I should not get beyond the statement that I had a new experience. It did not occur to me that the thing might be so well known, that a mere hint of the feelings concerned, would enable any older person to classify the consciousness. I said to myself I should merely perplex my uncle. And in truth I believe that love, in every mind in which it arises, will vary in colour and form—will always partake of that mind's individual isolation in difference. This, however, is nothing to the present point.

Comfort myself as I might, that the impossible was required of no one, and granted that the thing was impossible, it was none the less a cause of misery, a present disaster: I was aware, and soon my uncle would be aware, of an impenetrable something separating us. I felt that we had already begun to grow strange to each other, and the feeling lay like death at my heart.

Our lessons together were still going on; that I was no longer a child had made only the difference that progress must make; and I had no thought that they would not thus go on always. They were never for a moment irksome to me; I might be tired by them, but never of them. We were regularly at work together by seven, and after half an hour for breakfast, resumed work; at half-past eleven our lessons were over. But although the day was then clear of the imperative, much the greater part of it was in general passed in each other's company. We might not speak a word, but we would be hours together in the study. We might not speak a word, but we would be hours together on horseback.

For this day, then, our lessons were over, and my uncle was from home. This was an indisputable relief, yet the fact that it was so, pained me keenly, for I recognized in it the first of the schism. How I got through the day, I cannot tell. I was in a dream, not all a dream of delight. Haunted with the face I had seen, and living in the new consciousness it had waked in me, I spent most of it in the garden, now in the glooms of the yew-walks, and now in the smiling wilderness. It was odd, however, that, although I was not *expected* to be in my uncle's room at any time but that of lessons, all the morning I had a feeling as if I ought to be there, while yet glad that my uncle was not there.

It was late before he returned, and I went to bed. Perhaps I retired so soon that I might not have to look into his eyes. Usually, I sat now until he came home. I was long in getting to sleep, and then I dreamed. I thought I was out in the storm, and the flash came which revealed the horse and his rider, but they were both different. The horse in the dream was black as coal, as if carved out of the night itself; and the man upon him was the beautiful stranger whose horse I had not seen for the garden-wall. The darkness fell, and the voice of my uncle called to me. I waited for him in the storm with a troubled heart, for I knew he had not seen that vision, and I could no more tell him of it, than could Christabel tell her father what she had seen after she lay down. I woke, but my waking was no relief.

CHAPTER 11

The Mole Burrows

I SLEPT again after my dream, and do not know whether he came into my room as he generally did when he had not said good-night to me. Of course I woke unhappy, and the morning-world had lost something of its natural glow, its lovely freshness: it was not this time a thing new-born of the creating word. I dawdled with my dressing. The face kept coming, and brought me no peace, yet brought me something for which it seemed worth while even to lose my peace. But I did not know then, and do not yet know what the loss of peace actually means. I only know that it must be something far more terrible than anything I have ever known. I remained so far true to my uncle, however, that not even for what the face seemed to promise me, would I have consented to cause him trouble. For what I saw in the face, I would do anything, I thought, except that.

I went to him at the usual hour, determined that nothing should distract me from my work—that he should perceive no difference in me. I was not at the moment awake to the fact that here again were love and deception hand in hand. But another love than mine was there: my uncle loved me immeasurably more than I yet loved that heavenly vision. True love is keen-sighted as the eagle, and my uncle's love was love true, therefore he saw what I sought to hide. It is only the shadow of love, generally a grotesque, ugly thing, like so many other shadows, that is blind either to the troubles or the faults of the shadow it seems to love. The moment our eyes met, I saw that he saw something in mine that was not there when last we parted. But he said nothing, and we sat down to our lessons. Every now and then as they proceeded, however, I felt rather than saw his eyes rest on me for a moment, questioning. I had never known them rest on me so before. Plainly he was aware of some change; and could there be anything different in the relation of two who so long had loved each other, without something being less well and good than before? Nor was it indeed wonderful he should see a difference; for, with all the might of my resolve to do even better than usual, I would now and then find myself unconscious of what either of us had last been saying. The face had come yet again, and driven everything from its presence! I grew angry—not with the youth, but with his face, for appearing so often when I did not invite it. Once I caught myself on the verge of crying out, "Can't you wait? I will come presently!" and my uncle looked up as if I had spoken. Perhaps he had as good as heard the words; he possessed what almost seemed a supernatural faculty of divining the thought of another—not, I was sure, by any effort to perceive it, but by involuntary intuition. He uttered no inquiring word, but a light sigh escaped him, which all but made me burst into tears. I was on one side of a widening gulf, and he on the other!

Our lessons ended, he rose immediately and left the room. Five minutes passed, and then came the clatter of his horse's feet on the stones of the yard. A moment more, and I heard him ride away at a quick trot. I burst into tears where I still sat beside my uncle's empty chair. I was weary like one in a dream searching in vain for a spot whereupon to set down her heart-breaking burden. There was no one but my uncle to whom I could tell any trouble, and the trouble I could not have told him had hitherto been unimaginable! From this my reader may judge what a trouble it was that I could not tell him my trouble. I was a traitor to my only friend! Had I begun to love him less? had I begun to turn away from him? I dared not believe it. That would have been to give eternity to my misery. But it might be that at heart I was a bad, treacherous girl! I had again a secret from him! I was not *with* him!

I went into the garden. The day was sultry and oppressive. Coolness or comfort was nowhere. I sought the shadow of the live yew-walls; there was shelter in the shadow, but it oppressed the lungs while it comforted the eyes. Not a breath of wind breathed; the atmosphere seemed to have lost its life-giving. I went out into the wilderness. There the air was filled and heaped with the odours of the heavenly plants that crowded its humble floor, but they gave me no welcome. Between two bushes that flamed out roses, I lay down, and the heather and the rose-trees closed above me. My mind was in such a confusion of pain and pleasure—not without a hope of deliverance somewhere in its clouded sky—that I could think no more, and fell asleep.

I imagine that, had I never again seen the young man, I should not have suffered. I think that, by slow natural degrees, his phantasmal presence would have ceased to haunt me, and gradually I should have returned to my former condition. I do not mean I should have forgotten him, but neither should I have been troubled when I thought of him. I know I should never have regretted having seen him. In that, I had nothing to blame myself for, and should have felt—not that a glory had passed away from the earth, but that I had had a vision of bliss. What it was, I should not have had the power to recall, but it would have left with me the faith that I had beheld something too ethereal for my memory to store. I should have consoled myself both with the dream, and with the conviction that I should not dream it again. The peaceful sense of recovered nearness to my uncle would have been far more precious than the dream. The sudden fire of transfiguration that had for a moment flamed out of the All, and straightway withdrawn, would have become a memory only; but none the less would that enlargement of the child way of seeing things have remained with me. I do not think that would ever have left me: it is the care of the prudent wise that bleaches the grass, and is as the fumes of sulphur to the red rose of life.

Outwearied with inward conflict, I slept a dreamless sleep.

CHAPTER 12

A Letter

A COOL soft breeze went through the curtains of my couch, and I awoke. The blooms of the peasant-briars and the court-roses were waving together over my head. The sigh of the wind had breathed itself out over the far heath, and ere it died in my fairy forest of lowly plants and bushes, had found and fanned the cheeks that lay down hot and athirst for air. It gave me new life, and I rose refreshed. Something fluttered to the ground. I thought it was a leaf from a white rose above me, but I looked. At my feet lay a piece of paper. I took it up. It had been folded very hastily, and had no address, but who could have a better right to unfold it than I! It might be nothing; it might be a letter. Should I open it? Should I not rather seize the opportunity of setting things right between my heart and my uncle by taking it to him un-opened? Only, if it were indeed—I dared hardly even in thought complete the supposition—might it not be a wrong to the youth? Might not the paper contain a confidence? might it not be the messenger of a heart that trusted me before even it knew my name? Would I inaugurate our acquaintance with an act of treachery, or at least distrust? Right or wrong, thus my heart reasoned, and to its reasoning I gave heed. "It will," I said, "be time enough to resolve, when I know concerning what!" This, I now see, was juggling; for the question was whether I should be open with my uncle or not. "It might be," I said to myself, "that, the moment I knew the contents of the paper, I should reproach myself that I had not read it at once!"

I sat down on a bush of heather, and unfolded it. This is what I found, written with a pencil:—

"I am the man to whom you talked so kindly over your garden wall yesterday. I fear you may think me presuming and impertinent. Presuming I may be, but impertinent, surely not! If I were, would not my heart tell me so, seeing it is all on your side?

"My name is John Day; I do not yet know yours. I have not dared to inquire after it, lest I should hear of some impassable gulf between us. The fear of such a gulf haunts me. I can think of nothing but the face I saw over the wall through the clusters of lilac: the wall seems to keep rising and rising, as if it would hide you for ever.

"Is it wrong to think thus of you without your leave? If one may not love the loveliest, then is the world but a fly-trap hung in the great heaven, to catch and ruin souls!

"If I am writing nonsense—I cannot tell whether I am or not—it is because my wits wander with my eyes to gaze

at you through the leaves of the wild white rose under
which you are asleep. Loveliest of faces, may no gentlest
wind of thought ripple thy perfect calm, until I have said
what I must, and laid it where she will find it!

"I live at Rising, the manor-house over the heath. I am
the son of Lady Cairnedge by a former marriage. I am
twenty years of age, and have just ended my last term at
Oxford. May I come and see you? If you will not see me,
why then did you walk into my quiet house, and turn
everything upside down? I shall come to-night, in the
dusk, and wait in the heather, outside the fence. If you
come, thank God! if you do not, I shall believe you could
not, and come again and again and again, till hope is
dead. But I warn you I am a terrible hoper.

"It would startle, perhaps offend you, to wake and see
me; but I cannot bear to leave you asleep. Something
might come too near you. I will write until you move, and
then make haste to go.

"My heart swells with words too shy to go out. Surely
a Will has brought us together! I believe in fate, never
in chance!

"When we see each other again, will the wall be down
between us, or shall I know it will part us all our mortal
lives? Longer than that it cannot. If you say to me, 'I must
not see you, but I will think of you,' not one shall ever
know I have other than a light heart. Even now I begin
the endeavour to be such that, when we meet at last, as
meet we must, you shall not say, 'Is this the man, alas,
who dared to love me!'

"I love you as one might love a woman-angel who, at
the merest breath going to fashion a word unfit, would
spread her wings and soar. Do not, I pray you, fear to let

me come! There are things that must be done in faith, else they never have being: let this be one of them.—You stir."

As I came to these last words, hurriedly written, I heard behind me, over the height, the quick gallop of a horse, and knew the piece of firm turf he was crossing. The same moment I was there in spirit, and the imagination was almost vision. I saw him speeding away—"to come again!" said my heart, solemn with gladness.

Rising-manor was the house to which the lady took me that dread night when first I knew what it was to be alone in darkness and silence and space. Was that lady his mother? Had she rescued me for her son? I was not willing to believe it, though I had never actually seen her. The way was mostly dark, and during the latter portion of it, I was much too weary to look up where she sat on her great horse. I had never to my knowledge heard who lived at Rising. I was not born inquisitive, and there were miles between us.

I sat still, without impulse to move a finger. I lived essentially. Now I knew what had come to me. It was no merely idiosyncratic experience, for the youth had the same: it was love! How otherwise could we thus be drawn together from both sides! Verily it seemed also good enough to be that wondrous thing ever on the lips of poets and tale-weaving magicians! Was it not far beyond any notion of it their words had given me?

But my uncle! There lay bitterness! Was I indeed false to him, that now the thought of him was a pain? Had I begun a new life apart from him? To tell him would perhaps check the terrible separation! But how was I to tell him? For the first time I knew that I had no mother!

Would Mr. Day's mother be my mother too, and help me? But from no woman save my own mother, hardly even from her, would I ask mediation with the uncle I had loved and trusted all my life and with my whole heart. I had never known father or mother, save as he had been father and mother and everybody to me! What was I to do? Gladly would I have hurried to some desert place, and there waited for the light I needed. That I was no longer in any uncertainty as to the word that described my condition, did not, I found, make it easy to use the word. "Perhaps," I argued, struggling in the toils of my new liberty, "my uncle knows nothing of this kind of love, and would be unable to understand me! Suppose I confessed to him what I felt toward a man I had spoken to but once, and then only to tell him the way to Dumbleton, would he not think me out of my mind?"

At length I bethought me that, so long as I did not know what to do, I was not required to do anything; I must wait till I did know what to do. But with the thought came suffering enough to be the wages of any sin that, so far as I knew, I had ever committed. For the conviction awoke that already the love that had hitherto been the chief joy of my being, had begun to pale and fade. Was it possible I was ceasing to love my uncle? What could any love be worth if mine should fail my uncle! Love itself must be a mockery, and life but a ceaseless sliding down to the death of indifference! Even if I never ceased to love him, it was just as bad to love him less! Had he not been everything to me?—and this man, what had he ever done for me? Doubtless we are to love even our enemies; but are we to love them as tenderly as we love our friends? Or are we to love the friend of yesterday, of whom we know nothing though we may believe everything, as we love those who have taken all the trouble to make true men and women of us? "What can be the matter with my soul?" I said. "Can that soul be right made, in which one love begins to wither the moment another begins to grow? If I be so made, I cannot help being worthless!"

It was then first, I think, that I received a notion—anything like a true notion, that is, of my need of a God—whence afterward I came to see the one need of the whole race. Of course, not being able to make ourselves, it needed a God to make us; but that making were a small thing indeed, if he left us so unfinished that we could come to nothing right;—if he left us so that we could think or do or be nothing right;—if our souls were created so puny, for instance, that there was not room in them to love as they could not help loving, without ceasing to love where they were bound by every obligation to love right heartily, and more and more deeply! But had I not been growing all the time I had been in the world? There must then be the possibility of growing still! If there was not room in me, there must be room in God for me to become larger! The room in God must be made room in me! God had not done making me, in fact, and I sorely needed him to go on making me; I sorely needed to be made out! What if this new joy and this new terror had come, had been sent, in order to make me grow? At least the doors were open; I could go out and forsake myself! If a living power had caused me —and certainly I did not cause myself—then that living power knew all about me, knew every smallness that distressed me! Where should I find him? He could not be so far that the misery of one of his own children could not reach him! I turned my face into the grass, and prayed as I had never prayed before. I had always gone to church, and made the responses attentively, while I knew that was not praying, and tried to pray better than that; but now I was really asking from God something I sorely wanted. "Father in heaven," I said, "I am so miserable! Please, help me!"

I rose, went into the house, and up to the study, took a sock I was knitting for my uncle, and sat down to wait what would come. I could think no more; I could only wait.

CHAPTER 13

Old Love and New

W HILE I waited, as nearly a log, under the weariness of spiritual unrest, as a girl could well be, the door opened. Very seldom did that door open to any one but my uncle or myself: he would let no one but me touch his books, or even dust the room. I jumped from the chest where I sat.

It was only Martha Moon.

"How you startled me, Martha!" I cried.

"No wonder, child!" she answered. "I come with bad news! Your uncle has had a fall. He is laid up at Wittenage with a broken right arm."

I burst into tears.

"Oh, Martha!" I cried; "I must go to him!"

"He has sent for me," she answered quietly. "Dick is putting the horse to the phaeton."

"He doesn't want me, then!" I said; but it seemed a voice not my own that shrieked the words.

The punishment of my sin was upon me. Never would he have sent for Martha and not me, I thought, had he not seen that I had gone wrong again, and was no more to be trusted.

"My dear," said Martha, "which of us two ought to be the better nurse? You never saw your uncle ill; I've nursed him at death's door!"

"Then you don't think he is angry with me, Martha?" I said, humbled before myself.

"Was he ever angry with you, Orbie? What is there to be angry about? I never saw him even displeased with you!"

I had not realized that my uncle was suffering—only that he was disabled; now the fact flashed upon me, and with it the perception that I had been thinking only of myself: I was fast ceasing to care for him! And then, horrible to tell! a flash of joy went through me, that he would not be home that day, and therefore I *could* not tell him anything!

The moment Martha left me I threw myself on the floor of the desert room. I was in utter misery.

"Gladly would I bear every pang of his pain," I said to myself; "yet I have not asked one question about his accident! He must be in danger, or he would not have sent for Martha instead of me!"

How had the thing happened, I wondered. Had Death fallen with him—perhaps on him? He was such a horseman, I could not think he had been thrown. Besides, Death was a good horse who loved his master—dearly, I was sure, and would never have thrown him or let him fall! A great gush of the old love poured from the fountain in my heart: sympathy with the horse had unsealed it. I sprang from the floor, and ran down to entreat

Martha to take me with her: if my uncle did not want me, I could return with Dick! But she was gone. Even the sound of her wheels was gone. I had lain on the floor longer than I knew.

I went back to the study a little relieved. I understood now that I was not glad he was disabled; that I was anything but glad he was suffering; that I had only been glad for an instant that the crisis of my perplexity was postponed. In the meantime I should see John Day, who would help me to understand what I ought to do!

Very strange were my feelings that afternoon in the lonely house. I had always felt it lonely when Martha, never when my uncle was out. Yet when my uncle was in, I was mostly with him, and seldom more than a few minutes at a time with Martha. Our feelings are odd creatures! Now that both were away, there was neither time nor space in my heart for feeling the house desolate; while the world outside was rich as a treasure-house of mighty kings. The moment I was a little more comfortable with myself, my thoughts went in a flock to the face that looked over the garden-wall, to the man that watched me while I slept, the man that wrote that lovely letter. Inside was old Penny with her broom: she took advantage of every absence to sweep or scour or dust; outside was John Day, and the roses of the wilderness! He was waiting the hour to come to me, wondering how I would receive him!

Slowly went the afternoon. I had fallen in love at first sight, it is true; not therefore was I eager to meet my lover. I was only more than willing to see him. It was as sweet, or nearly as sweet, to dream of his coming, as to have him before me—so long as I knew he was indeed coming. I was just a little anxious lest I should not find him altogether so beautiful as I was imagining him. That he was good, I never doubted: could I otherwise have fallen in love with him? And his letter was so straightforward—so manly!

The afternoon was cloudy, and the twilight came the sooner. From the realms of the dark, where all the birds of night build their nests, lining them with their own sooty down, the sweet odorous filmy dusk of the summer, haunted with wings of noiseless bats, began at length to come flickering earthward, in a snow infinitesimal of fluffiest gray and black: I crept out into the garden. It was dark as wintry night among the yews, but I could have gone any time through every alley of them blindfolded. An owl cried and I started, for my soul was sunk in its own love-dawn. There came a sudden sense of light as I opened the door into the wilderness, but light how thin and pale, and how full of expectation! The earth and the vast air, up to the great vault, seemed to throb and heave with life—or was it that my spirit lay an open thoroughfare to the life of the All? With the scent of the roses and the humbler sweet-odoured inhabitants of the wilderness; with the sound of the brook that ran through it, flowing from the heath and down the hill; with the silent starbeams, and the insects that make all the little noises they can; with the thoughts that went out of me, and returned possessed of the earth;—with all these, and the sense of thought eternal, the universe was full as it could hold. I stood in the doorway of the wall, and looked out on the wild: suddenly, by some strange reaction, it seemed out of creation's doors, out in the illimitable, given up to the bare, to the space that had no

walls! A shiver ran through me; I turned back among the
yews. It was early; I would wait yet a while! If he were
already there, he too would enjoy the calm of a lovely
little wait.

A small wind came searching about, and found, and
caressed me. I turned to it; it played with my hair, and
cooled my face. After a while, I left the alley, passed out,
closed the door behind me, and went straying through
the broken ground of the wilderness, among the low
bushes, meandering, as if with some frolicsome brook
for a companion—a brook of capricious windings—but
still coming nearer to the fence that parted the wilderness from the heath, my eyes bent down, partly to avoid
the hillocks and bushes, and partly from shyness of the
moment when first I should see him who was in my heart
and somewhere near. Softly the moon rose, round and
full. There was still so much light in the sky that she
made no sudden change, and for a moment I did not feel
her presence or look up. In front of me, the high ground
of the moor sank into a hollow, deeply indenting the
horizon-line: the moon was rising just in the gap, and
when I did look up, the lower edge of her disc was just
clear of the earth, and the head of a man looking over the
fence was in the middle of the great moon. It was like the
head of a saint in a missal, girt with a halo of solid gold.
I could not see the face, for the halo hid it, as such
attributions are apt to do, but it must be he; and
strengthened by the heavenly vision, I went toward him.
Walking less carefully than before, however, I caught my
foot, stumbled, and fell. There came a rush through the
bushes; he was by my side, lifted me like a child, and held
me in his arms; neither was I more frightened than a

child caught up in the arms of any well-known friend: I had been bred in faith and not mistrust! But indeed my head had struck the ground with such force, that, had I been inclined, I could scarcely have resisted—though why should I have resisted, being where I would be! Does not philosophy tell us that growth and development, cause and effect, are all, and that the days and years are of no account? And does not more than philosophy tell us that truth is everything?"

"My darling! Are you hurt?" murmured the voice whose echoes seemed to have haunted me for centuries.

"A little," I answered. "I shall be all right in a minute." I did not add, "Put me down, please;" for I did not want to be put down directly. I could not have stood if he had put me down. I grew faint.

Life came back, and I felt myself growing heavy in his arms.

"I think I can stand now," I said. "Please put me down."

He obeyed immediately.

"I've nearly broken your arms," I said, ashamed of having become a burden to him the moment we met.

"I could run with you to the top of the hill!" he answered.

"I don't think you could," I returned.

Perhaps I leaned a little toward him; I do not know. He put his arm round me.

"You are not able to stand," he said. "Shall we sit a moment?"

CHAPTER 14

Mother and Uncle

I WAS glad enough to sink on a clump of white clover. He stretched himself on the heather, a little way from me. Silence followed. He was giving me time to recover myself. As soon, therefore, as I was able, it was my part to speak.

"Where is your horse?" I asked.

The first word is generally one hardly worth saying.

"I left him at a little farmhouse, about a mile from here. I was afraid to bring him farther, lest my mother should learn where I had been. She takes pains to know."

"Then will she not find out?"

"I don't know."

"Will she not ask you where you were?"

"Perhaps. There's no knowing."

"You will tell her, of course, if she does?"

"I think not."

"Oughtn't you?"

"No."

"You are sure?"

"Yes."

"You don't mean you will tell her a story?"

"Certainly not."

"What will you do then?"

"I will tell her that I will not tell her."

"Would that be right?"

Through the dusk I could see the light of his smile as he answered.

"I think so. I shall not tell her."

"But," I began.

He interrupted me.

My heart was sinking within me. Not only had I wanted him to help me to tell my uncle, but I shuddered at the idea of having with any man a secret from his mother.

"It must look strange to you," he said; "but you do not know my mother!"

"I think I do know your mother," I rejoined. "She saved my poor little life once.—I am not sure it was your mother, but I think it was."

"How was that?" he said, much surprised. "When was it?"

"Many years ago—I cannot tell how many," I answered. "But I remember all about it well enough. I cannot have been more than eight, I imagine."

"Could she have been at the manor then?" he said, putting the question to himself, not me. "How was it? Tell me," he went on, rising to his feet, and looking at me with almost a frightened expression.

I told him the incident, and he heard me in absolute silence. When I had done,—

"It *was* my mother!" he broke out; "I don't know one other woman who would have let a child walk like that! Any other would have taken you up, or put you on the horse and walked beside you!"

"A gentleman would, I know," I replied. "But it would not be so easy for a lady!"

"*She* could have done either well enough. She's as strong as a horse herself, and rides like an Amazon. But I am not in the least surprised: it was just like her! You poor little darling! It nearly makes me cry to think of the tiny feet going tramp, tramp, all that horrible way, and she high up on her big horse! She always rides the biggest horse she can get!—And then never to say a word to you after she brought you home, or see you the next morning!"

"Mr. Day," I returned, "I would not have told you, had I known it would give you occasion to speak so naughtily of your mother. You make me unhappy."

He was silent. I thought he was ashamed of himself, and was sorry for him. But my sympathy was wasted. He broke into a murmuring laugh of merriment.

"When is a mother not a mother?" he said. "—Do you give it up?—When she's a north wind. When she's a Roman emperor. When she's an iceberg. When she's a brass tiger.—There! that'll do. Good-bye, mother, for the present! I mayn't know much, as she's always telling me, but I do know that a noun is not a thing, nor a name a person!"

I would have expostulated.

"For love's sake, dearest," he pleaded, "we will not

dispute where only one of us knows! I will tell you all some day—soon, I hope, very soon. I am angry now!—Poor little tramping child!"

I saw I had been behaving presumptuously: I had wanted to argue while yet in absolute ignorance of the thing in hand! Had not my uncle taught me the folly of reasoning from the ideal where I knew nothing of the actual! The ideal must be our guide how to treat the actual, but the actual must be there to treat! One thing more I saw—that there could be no likeness between his mother and my uncle!

"Will you tell me something about yourself, then?" I said.

"That would not be interesting!" he objected.

"Then why are you here?" I returned. "Can any person without a history be interesting?"

"Yes," he answered: "a person that was going to have a history might be interesting."

"Could a person with a history that was not worth telling, be interesting? But I know yours will interest me in the hearing, therefore it ought to interest you in the telling."

"I see," he rejoined, with his merry laugh, "I shall have to be careful! My lady will at once pounce upon the weak points of my logic!"

"I am no logician," I answered; "I only know when I don't know a thing. My uncle has taught me that wisdom lies in that."

"Yours must be a very unusual kind of uncle!" he returned.

"If God had made many men like my uncle, I think the world wouldn't be the same place."

"I wonder why he didn't!" he said thoughtfully.

"I have wondered much, and cannot tell," I replied.

"What if it wouldn't be good for the world to have many good men in it before it was ready to treat them properly?" he suggested.

The words let me know that at least he could think. Hitherto my uncle had seemed to me the only man that thought. But I had seen very few men.

"Perhaps that is it," I answered. "I will think about it. —Were you brought up at Rising? Have you been there all the time? Were you there that night? I should surely have known had you been in the house!"

He looked at me with a grateful smile.

"I was not brought up there," he answered. "Rising is mine, however—at least it will be when I come of age; it was left me some ten years ago by a great-aunt. My father's property will be mine too, of course. My mother's is in Ireland. She ought to be there, not here; but she likes my estates better than her own, and makes the most of being my guardian."

"You would not have her there if she is happier here?"

"All who have land, ought to live on it, or else give it to those who will. What makes it theirs, if their only connection with it is the money it brings them? If I let my horse run wild over the country, how could I claim him, and refuse to pay his damages?"

"I don't quite understand you."

"I only mean there is no bond where both ends are not tied. My mother has no sense of obligation, so far as ever I have been able to see. But do not be afraid: I would as soon take a wife to the house she was in, as I would ask her to creep with me into the den of a hyena."

It was too dreadful! I rose. He sprang to his feet.

"You must excuse me, sir!" I said. "With one who can speak so of his mother, I am where I ought not to be."

"You have a right to know what my mother is," he answered—coldly, I thought; "and I should not be a true man if I spoke of her otherwise than truly."

He would pretend nothing to please me! I saw that I was again in the wrong. Was I so ill read as to imagine that a mother must of necessity be a good woman? Was he to speak of his mother as he did not believe of her, or be unfit for my company? Would untruth be a bond between us?

"I beg your pardon," I said; "I was wrong. But you can hardly wonder I should be shocked to hear a son speak so of his mother—and to one all but a stranger!"

"What!" he returned, with a look of surprise; "do you think of me so? I feel as if I had known you all my life —and before it!"

I felt ashamed, and was silent. If he was such a stranger, why was I there alone with him?

"You must not think I speak so to *any* one," he went on. "Of those who know my mother, not one has a right to demand of me anything concerning her. But how could I ask you to see me, and hide from you the truth about her? Prudence would tell you to have nothing to do with the son of such a woman: could I be a true man, true to you, and hold my tongue about her? I should be a liar of the worst sort!"

He felt far too strongly, it was plain, to heed a world of commonplaces.

"Forgive me," I said. "May I sit down again?"

He held out his hand. I took it, and reseated myself on

the clover-hillock. He laid himself again beside me, and after a little silence began to relate what occurred to him of his external history, while all the time I was watching for hints as to how he had come to be the man he was. It was clear he did not find it easy to talk about himself. But soon I no longer doubted whether I ought to have met him, and loved him a great deal more by the time he had done.

I then told him in return what my life had hitherto been; how I knew nothing of father or mother; how my uncle had been everything to me; how he had taught me all I knew, had helped me to love what was good and hate what was evil, had enabled me to value good books, and turn away from foolish ones. In short, I made him feel that all his mother had not been to him, my uncle had been to me; and that it would take a long time to make me as much indebted to a husband as already I was to my uncle. Then I put the question:

"What would you think of me if I had a secret from an uncle like that?"

"If I had an uncle like that," he answered, "I would sooner cut my throat than keep anything from him!"

"I have not told him," I said, "what happened to-day —or yesterday."

"But you will tell him?"

"The first moment I can. But I hope you understand it is hard to do. My love for my uncle makes it hard. It has the look of turning away from him to love another!"

With that I burst out crying. I could not help it. He let me cry, and did not interfere. I was grateful for that. When at length I raised my head, he spoke.

"It has that look," he said; "but I trust it is only a look.

Anyhow, he knows that such things must be; and the more of a good man and a gentleman he is, the less will he be pained that we should love one another!"

"I am sure of that," I replied. "I am only afraid that he may never have been in love himself, and does not know how it feels, and may think I have forsaken him for you."

"Are you with him *always?*"

"No; I am sometimes a good deal alone. I can be alone as much as I like; he always gives me perfect liberty. But I never before wanted to be alone when I could be with him."

"But he *could* live without you?"

"Yes, indeed!" I cried. "He would be a poor creature that could not live without another!"

He said nothing, and I added,

"He often goes out alone—sometimes in the darkest nights."

"Then be sure he knows what love is.—But, if you would rather, I will tell him."

"I could not have any one, even you, tell my uncle about me."

"You are right. When will you tell him?"

"I cannot be sure. I would go to him tomorrow, but I am afraid they will not let me until he has got a little over this accident," I answered—and told him what had happened. "It is dreadful to think how he must have suffered," I said, "and how much more I should have thought about it but for you! It tears my heart. Why wasn't it made bigger?"

"Perhaps that is just what is now being done with it!" he answered.

"I hope it may be!" I returned. "—But it is time I went in."

"Shall I not see you again to-morrow evening?" he asked.

"No," I answered. "I must not see you again till I have told my uncle everything."

"You do not mean for weeks and weeks—till he is well enough to come home? How *am* I to live till then!"

"As I shall have to live. But I hope it will be but for a few days at most. Only, then, it will depend on what my uncle thinks of the thing."

"Will he decide for you what you are to do?"

"Yes—I think so. Perhaps if he were——"

I was on the point of saying, "like your mother," but I stopped in time—or hardly, for I think he saw what I just saved myself from.

It was but the other morning I made the discovery that, all our life together, John has never once pressed me to complete a sentence I broke off.

He looked so sorrowful that I was driven to add something.

"I don't think there is much good," I said, "in resolving what you will or will not do, before the occasion appears, for it may have something in it you never reckoned on. All I can say is, I will try to do what is right. I cannot promise anything without knowing what my uncle thinks."

We rose; he took me in his arms for just an instant; and we parted with the understanding that I was to write to him as soon as I had spoken with my uncle.

CHAPTER 15

The Time Between

I NOW felt quite able to confess to my uncle both what I had thought and what I had done. True, I had much more to confess than when my trouble first awoke; but the growth in the matter of the confession had been such a growth in definiteness as well, as to make its utterance, though more weighty, yet much easier. If I might be in doubt about revealing my thoughts, I could be in none about revealing my actions; and I found it was much less appalling to make known my feelings, when I had the words of John Day to confess as well.

I may here be allowed to remark, how much easier an action is when demanded, than it seems while in the contingent future—how much easier when the thing is before you in its reality, and not as a mere thought-spectre. The thing itself, and the idea of it, are two such different grounds upon which to come either to a decision or to action!

One thing more: when a woman wants to do the right
—I do not mean, wants to coax the right to side with her
—she will, somehow, be led up to it.

My uncle was very feverish and troubled the first night,
and had a good deal of delirium, during which his care
and anxiety seemed all about me. Martha had to assure
him every other moment that I was well, and in no danger of any sort: he would be silent for a time, and then
again show himself tormented with forebodings about
me. In the morning, however, he was better; only he
looked sadder than usual. She thought he was, for some
cause or other, in reality anxious about me. So much I
gathered from Martha's letter, by no means scholarly,
but graphic enough.

It gave me much pain. My uncle was miserable about
me: he had plainly seen, he knew and felt that something
had come between us! Alas, it was no fancy of his brain-
troubled soul! Whether I was in fault or not, there was
that something! It troubled the unity that had hitherto
seemed a thing essential and indivisible!

Dared I go to him without a summons? I knew Martha
would call me the moment the doctor allowed her: it
would not be right to go without that call. What I had to
tell might justify far more anxiety than the sight of me
would counteract. If I said nothing, the keen eye of his
love would assure itself of the something hid in my silence, and he would not see that I was but waiting his
improvement to tell him everything. I resolved therefore
to remain where I was.

The next two days were perhaps the most uncomfort-
able ever I spent. A secret one desires to turn out of
doors at the first opportunity, is not a pleasant compan-

ion. I do not say I was unhappy, still less that once I wished I had not seen John Day, but oh, how I longed to love him openly! how I longed for my uncle's sanction, without which our love could not be perfected! Then John's mother was by no means a gladsome thought—except that he must be a good man indeed, who was good in spite of being unable to love, respect, or trust his mother! The true notion of heaven, is to be with everybody one loves: to him the presence of his mother—such as she was, that is—would destroy any heaven! What a painful but salutary shock it will be to those whose existence is such a glorifying of themselves that they imagine their presence necessary to all about them, when they learn that their disappearance from the world sent a thrill of relief through the hearts of those nearest them! To learn how little they were prized, will one day prove a strong medicine for souls self-absorbed.

"There is nothing covered that shall not be revealed."

CHAPTER 16

Fault and No Fault

THE next day I kept the house till the evening, and then went walking in the garden in the twilight. Between the dark alleys and the open wilderness I flitted and wandered, alternating gloom and gleam outside me, even as they chased one another within me.

In the wilderness I looked up—and there was John! He stood outside the fence, just as I had seen him the night before, only now there was no aureole about his head: the moon had not yet reached the horizon.

My first feeling was anger: he had broken our agreement! I did not reflect that there was such a thing as breaking a law, or even a promise, and being blameless. He leaped the fence, and clearing every bush like a deer, came straight toward me. It was no use trying to escape him. I turned my back, and stood. He stopped close behind me, a yard or two away.

"Will you not speak to me?" he said. "It is not my fault I am come."

"Whose fault then, pray?" I rejoined, with difficulty keeping my position. "Is it mine?"

"My mother's," he answered.

I turned and looked him in the eyes, through the dusk saw that he was troubled, ran to him, and put my arms about him.

"She has been spying," he said, as soon as he could speak. "She will part us at any risk, if she can. She is having us watched this very moment, most likely. She may be watching us herself. She is a terrible woman when she is for or against anything. Literally, I do not know what she would not do to get her own way. She lives for her own way. The loss of it would be to her as the loss of her soul. She will lose it this time though! She will fail this time—if she never did before!"

"Well," I returned, nowise inclined to take her part, "I hope she will fail! What does she say?"

"She says she would rather go to her grave than see me your husband."

"Why?"

"Your family seems objectionable to her."

"What is there against it?"

"Nothing that I know."

"What is there against my uncle? Is there anything against Martha Moon?" I was indignant at the idea of a whisper against either. "What have *I* done?" I went on. "We are all of the family I know: what is it?"

"I don't think she has had time to invent anything yet;

but she pretends there is something, and says if I don't give you up, if I don't swear never to look at you again, she will tell it."

"What did you answer her?"

"I said no power on earth should make me give you up. Whatever she knew, she could know nothing against *you,* and I was as ready to go to my grave as she was. 'Mother,' I said, 'you may tell my determination by your own! Whether I marry her or not, you and I part company the day I come of age; and if you speak word or do deed against one of her family, my lawyer shall look strictly into your accounts as my guardian.' You see I knew where to touch her!"

"It is dreadful you should have to speak like that to your mother!"

"It is; but you would feel to her just as I do if you knew all—though you wouldn't speak so roughly, I know."

"Can you guess what she has in her mind?"

"Not in the least. She will pretend anything. It is enough that she is determined to part us. How, she cares nothing, so she succeed."

"But she cannot!"

"It rests with you."

"How with me?"

"It will be war to the knife between her and me. If she succeed, it must be with you. I will do anything to foil her except lie."

"What if she should make you see it your duty to give me up?"

"What if there were no difference between right and wrong! We're as good as married!"

"Yes, of course; but I cannot quite promise, you know, until I hear what my uncle will say."

"If your uncle is half so good a man as you have made me think him, he will do what he can on our side. He loves what is fair; and what can be fairer than that those who love each other should marry?"

I knew my uncle would not willingly interfere with my happiness, and for myself, I should never marry another than John Day—that was a thing of course: had he not kissed me? But the best of lovers had been parted, and that which had been might be again, though I could not see how! It *was* good, nevertheless, to hear John talk! It was the right way for a lover to talk! Still, he had no supremacy over what was to be!

"Some would say it cannot be so great a matter to us, when we have known each other such a little while!" I remarked.

"The true time is the long time!" he replied. "Would it be a sign that our love was strong, that it took a great while to come to anything? The strongest things—"

There he stopped, and I saw why: strongest things are not generally of quickest growth! But there was the eucalyptus! And was not St. Paul as good a Christian as any of them? I said nothing, however: there was indeed no rule in the matter!

"You must allow it possible," I said, "that we may not be married!"

"I will not," he answered. "It is true my mother may get me brought in as incapable of managing my own affairs; but—"

"What mother would do such a wicked thing!" I cried.

"*My* mother," he answered.

"Oh!"

"She *would!*"

"I can't believe it."

"I am sure of it."

I held my peace. I could not help a sense of dismay at finding myself so near such a woman. I knew of bad women, but only in books: it would appear they were in other places as well!

"We must be on our guard," he said.

"Against what?"

"I don't know; whatever she may do."

"We can't do anything till she begins!"

"She has begun."

"How?" I asked incredulous.

"Leander is lame," he answered.

"I am so sorry!"

"I am so angry!"

"Is it possible I understand you?"

"Quite. *She* did it."

"How do you know?"

"I can no more prove it than I can doubt it. I cannot inquire into my mother's proceedings. I leave that sort of thing to her. Let her spy on me as she will, I am not going to spy on her."

"Of course not! But if you have no proof, how can you state the thing as a fact?"

"I have what is proof enough for saying it to my own soul."

"But you have spoken of it to me!"

"You are my better soul. If you are not, then I have done wrong in saying it to you."

I hastened to tell him I had only made him say what

I hoped he meant—only I wasn't his *better* soul. He wanted me then to promise that I would marry him in spite of any and every thing. I promised that I would never marry any one but him. I could not say more, I said, not knowing what my uncle might think, but so much it was only fair to say. For I had gone so far as to let him know distinctly that I loved him; and what sort would that love be that could regard it as possible, at any distance of time, to marry another! or what sort of woman could she be that would shrink from such a pledge! The mischief lies in promises made without fore-casting thought. I knew what I was about. I saw forward and backward and all around me. A solitary education opens eyes that, in the midst of companions and engage-ments, are apt to remain shut. Knowledge of the world is no safeguard to man or woman. In the knowledge and love of truth, lies our only safety.

With that promise he had to be, and was, content.

CHAPTER 17

The Summons

‸

Next morning the post brought me the following letter from my uncle. Whoever of my readers may care to enter into my feelings as I read, must imagine them for herself: I will not attempt to describe them. The letter was not easy to read, as it was written in bed, and with his left hand.

"My little one,—I think I know more than you imagine. I think the secret flew into your heart of itself; you did not take it up and put it there. I think you tried to drive it out, and it would not go: the same Fate that clips the thread of life, had clipped its wings that it could fly no more! Did my little one think I had not a heart big enough to hold her secret? I wish it had not been so: it has made her suffer! I pray my little one to be sure that I am all on her side; that my will is to do and contrive the best for her that lies in my power.

Should I be unable to do what she would like, she must yet believe me true to her as to my God, less than whom only I love her:—less, because God is so much bigger, that so much more love will hang upon him. I love you, dear, more than any other creature except one, and that one is not in this world. Be sure that, whatever it may cost me, I will be to you what your own perfected soul will approve. Not to do my best for you, would be to be false, not to God only, but to your father as well, whom I loved and love dearly. Come to me, my child, and tell me all. I know you have done nothing wrong, nothing to be ashamed of. Some things are so difficult to tell, that it needs help to make way for them: I will help you. I am better. Come to me at once, and we will break the creature's shell together, and see what it is like, the shy thing!—Your uncle."

I was so eager to go to him, that it was with difficulty I finished his letter before starting. Death had been sent home, and was in the stable, sorely missing his master. I called Dick, and told him to get ready to ride with me to Wittenage; he must take Thanatos, and be at the door with Zoe in twenty minutes.

We started. As we left the gate, I caught sight of John coming from the other direction, his eyes on the ground, lost in meditation. I stopped. He looked up, saw me, and was at my side in two moments.

"I have heard from my uncle," I said. "He wants me. I am going to him."

"If only I had my horse!" he answered.

"Why shouldn't you take Thanatos?" I rejoined.

"No," he answered, after a moment's hesitation. "It would be an impertinence. I will walk, and perhaps see

you there. It's only sixteen miles, I think.—What a splendid creature he is!"

"He's getting into years now," I replied; "but he has
been in the stable several days, and I am doubtful
whether Dick will feel quite at home on him."

"Then your uncle would rather I rode him! He knows
I am no tailor!" said John.

"How?" I asked.

"I don't mean he knows who I am, but he saw me a
fortnight ago, in one of our fields, giving Leander, who
is but three, a lesson or two. He stopped and looked on
for a good many minutes, and said a kind word about my
handling of the horse. He will remember, I am sure."

"How glad I am he knows something of you! If you
don't mind being seen with me, then, there is no reason
why you should not give me your escort."

Dick was not sorry to dismount, and we rode away
together.

I was glad of this for one definite reason, as well as
many indefinite: I wanted John to see my letter, and
know what cause I had to love my uncle. I forgot for the
moment my resolution not to meet him again before
telling my uncle everything. Somehow he seemed to be
going with me to receive my uncle's approval.

He read the letter, old Death carrying him all the time
as gently as he carried myself—I often rode him now—
and returned it with the tears in his eyes. For a moment
or two he did not speak. Then he said in a very solemn
way,

"I see! I oughtn't to have a chance if he be against me!
I understand now why I could not get you to promise!
—All right! The Lord have mercy upon me!"

"That he will! He is always having mercy upon us!" I answered, loving John and my uncle and God more than ever. I loved John for this especially, at the moment—that his nature remained uninjured toward others by his distrust of her who should have had the first claim on his confidence. I said to myself that, if a man had a bad mother and yet was a good man, there could be no limit to the goodness he must come to. That he was a man after my uncle's own heart, I had no longer the least doubt. Nor was it a small thing to me that he rode beautifully—never seeming to heed his horse, and yet in constant touch with him.

We reached the town, and the inn where my uncle was lying. On the road we had arranged where he would be waiting me to hear what came next. He went to see the horses put up, and I ran to find Martha. She met me on the stair, and went straight to my uncle to tell him I was come, returned almost immediately, and led me to his room.

I was shocked to see how pale and ill he looked. I feared, and was right in fearing, that anxiety about myself had not a little to do with his condition. His face brightened when he saw me, but his eyes gazed into mine with a searching inquiry. His face brightened yet more when he found his eager look answered by the smile which my perfect satisfaction inspired. I knelt by the bedside, afraid to touch him lest I should hurt his arm.

Slowly he laid his left hand on my head, and I knew he blessed me silently. For a minute or two he lay still.

"Now tell me all about it," he said at length, turning his patient blue eyes on mine.

I began at once, and if I did not tell him all, I let it be

plain there was more of the sort behind, concerning which he might question me. When I had ended,

"Is that everything?" he asked, with a smile so like all he had ever been to me, that my whole heart seemed to go out to meet it.

"Yes, uncle," I answered; "I think I may say so—except that I have not dwelt upon my feelings. Love, they say, is shy; and I fancy you will pardon me that portion."

"Willingly, my child. More is quite unnecessary."

"Then you know all about it, uncle?" I ventured. "I was afraid you might not understand me. Could any one, do you think, that had not had the same experience?"

He made me no answer. I looked up. He was ghastly white; his head had fallen back against the bed. I started up, hardly smothering a shriek.

"What is it, uncle?" I gasped. "Shall I fetch Martha?"

"No, my child," he answered. "I shall be better in a moment. I am subject to little attacks of the heart, but they do not mean much. Give me some of that medicine on the table."

In a few minutes his colour began to return, and the smile which was forced at first, gradually brightened until it was genuine.

"I will tell you the whole story one day," he said, "—whether in this world, I am doubtful. But *when* is nothing, or *where*, with eternity before us."

"Yes, uncle," I answered vaguely, as I knelt again by the bedside.

"A person," he said, after a while, slowly, and with hesitating effort, "may look and feel a much better person at one time than at another. Upon occasion, he is so happy, or perhaps so well pleased with himself, that the good in him comes all to the surface."

"Would he be the better or the worse man if it did not, uncle?" I asked.

"You must not get me into a metaphysical discussion, little one," he answered. "We have something more important on our hands. I want you to note that, when a person is happy, he may look lovable; whereas, things going as he does not like, another, and very unfinished phase of his character may appear."

"Surely everybody must know that, uncle!"

"Then you can hardly expect me to be confident that your new friend would appear as lovable if he were unhappy!"

"I have seen you, uncle, look as if nothing would ever make you smile again; but I knew you loved me all the time."

"Did you, my darling? Then you were right. *I* dare not require of any man that he should be as good-tempered in trouble as out of it—though he must come to that at last; but a man must be *just,* whatever mood he is in."

"That is what I always knew you to be, uncle! I never waited for a change in your looks, to tell you anything I wanted to tell you.—I know you, uncle!" I added, with a glow of still triumph.

"Thank you, little one!" he returned, half playfully, yet gravely. "All I want to say comes to this," he resumed after a pause, "that when a man is in love, you see only the best of him, or something better than he really is. Much good may be in a man, for God made him, and the man yet not be good, for he has done nothing, since his making, to make himself. Before you can say you know a man, you must have seen him in a few at least of his opposite moods. Therefore you cannot wonder that I should desire a fuller assurance of this young man, than your testimony, founded on an acquaintance of three or four days, can give me."

"Let me tell you, then, something that happened to-day," I answered. "When first I asked him to come with me this morning, it was a temptation to him of course, not knowing when we might see each other again; but he hadn't his own horse, and said it would be an impertinence to ride yours."

"I hope you did not come alone!"

"Oh, no. I had set out with Dick, but John came after all."

"Then his refusal to ride my horse does not come to much. It is a small thing to have good impulses, if temptation is too much for them."

"But I haven't done telling you, uncle!"

"I am hasty, little one. I beg your pardon."

"I have to tell you what made him give in to riding your horse. I confessed I was a little anxious lest Death, who had not been exercised for some days, should be too much for Dick. John said then he thought he might venture, for you had once spoken very kindly to him of the way he handled his own horse."

"Oh, that's the young fellow, is it!" cried my uncle, in a tone that could not be taken for other than one of pleasure. "That's the fellow, is it?" he repeated. "H'm!"

"I hope you liked the look of him, uncle!" I said.

"The boy is a gentleman anyhow!" he answered.— You may think whether I was pleased!—"I never saw man carry himself better horseward!" he added with a smile.

"Then you won't object to his riding Death home again?"

"Not in the least!" he replied. "The man can ride."

"And may I go with him?—that is, if you do not want me!—I wish I could stay with you!"

"Rather than ride home with him?"

"Yes, indeed, if it were to be of use to you!"

"The only way you can be of use to me, is to ride home with Mr. Day, and not see him again until I have had a little talk with him. Tyranny may be a sense of duty, you know, little one!"

"Tyranny, uncle!" I cried, as I laid my cheek to his hand, which was very cold. "You *could* not make me think you a tyrant!"

"I should not like you to think me one, darling! Still less would I like to deserve it, whether you thought me one or not! But I could not be a tyrant to you if I would. You may defy me when you please."

"That would be to poison my own soul!" I answered.

"You must understand," he continued, "that I have no authority over you. If you were going to marry Mr. Day to-morrow, I should have no right to interfere. I am but a makeshift father to you, not a legal guardian."

"Don't cast me off, uncle!" I cried. "You *know* I belong to you as much as if you were my very own father! I am sure my father will say so when we see him. He will never come between you and me."

He gave a great sigh, and his face grew so intense that I felt as if I had no right to look on it.

"It is one of the deepest hopes of my existence," he

said, "to give you back to him the best of daughters. Be good, my darling, be good, even if you die of sorrow because of it."

The intensity had faded to a deep sadness, and there came a silence.

"Would you like me to go now, uncle?" I asked.

"I wish I could see Mr. Day at once," he returned, "but I am so far from strong, that I fear both weakness and injustice. Tell him I want very much to see him, and will let him know as soon as I am able."

"Thank you, uncle! He will be so glad! Of course he can't feel as I do, but he does feel that to do anything you did not like, would be just horrid."

"And you will not see him again, little one, after he has taken you home, till I have had some talk with him?"

"Of course I will not, uncle."

I bade him good-bye, had a few moments' conference with Martha, and found John at the place appointed.

CHAPTER 18

John Sees Something

✦

As we rode, I told him everything. It did not seem in
the least strange that I should be so close to one of whom
a few days before I had never heard; it seemed as if all
my life I had been waiting for him, and now he was come,
and everything was only as it should be! We were very
quiet in our gladness. Some slight anxiety about my
uncle's decision, and the certain foreboding of trouble
on the part of his mother, stilled us both, sending the
delight of having found each other a little deeper and out
of the way of the practical and reasoning.

We did not urge our horses to their speed, but I felt
that, for my uncle's sake, I must not prolong the journey,
forcing the last farthing of bliss from his generosity,
while yet he was uncertain of his duty. The moon was
rising just as we reached my home, and I was glad: John
would have to walk miles to reach his, for he absolutely

refused to take Death on, saying he did not know what might happen to him. As we stopped at the gate I bethought myself that neither of us had eaten since we left in the afternoon. I dismounted, and leaving him with the horses, got what I could find for him, and then roused Dick, who was asleep. John confessed that, now I had made him think of it, he was hungry enough to eat anything less than an ox. We parted merrily, but when next we met, each confessed it had not been without a presentiment of impending danger. For my part, notwithstanding the position I had presumed to take with John when first he spoke of his mother, I was not as distrustful as he, and more afraid of her.

Much the nearest way between the two houses lay across the heath. John walked along, eating the supper I had given him, and now and then casting a glance round the horizon. He had got about half-way, when, looking up, he thought he saw, dim in the ghosty light of the moon, a speck upon the track before him. He said to himself it could hardly be any one on the moor at such a time of the night, and went on with his supper. Looking up again after an interval, he saw that the object was much larger, but hardly less vague, because of a light fog which had in the meantime risen. By and by, however, as they drew nearer to each other, a strange thrill of recognition went through him: on the way before him, which was little better than a footpath, and slowly approaching, came what certainly could be neither the horse that had carried him that day, nor his double, but what was so like him in colour, size, and bone, while so unlike him in muscle and bearing, that he might have been he, worn but for his skin to a skeleton. Straight down upon John he came, spectral through the fog, as if he were asleep, and saw nothing in his way. John stepped aside to let him pass, and then first looked in the face of his rider: with a shock of fear that struck him in the middle of the body, making him gasp and choke, he saw before him—so plainly that, but for the impossibility, he could have sworn to him in any court of justice—the man whom he knew to be at that moment confined to his bed, twenty miles away, with a broken arm. Sole other human being within sight or sound in that still moonlight, on that desolate moor, the horseman never lifted his head, never raised his eyes to look at him. John stood stunned. He hardly doubted he saw an apparition. When at length he roused himself, and looked in the direction in which it went, it had all but vanished in the thickening white mist.

He found the rest of his way home almost mechanically, and went straight to bed, but for a long time could not sleep.

For what might not the apparition portend? Mr. Whichcote lay hurt by a fall from his horse, and he had met his very image on the back of just such a horse, only turned to a skeleton! Was he bearing him away to the tomb?

Then he remembered that the horse's name was Death.

CHAPTER 19

John Is Taken Ill

IN the middle of the night he woke with a start, ill enough to feel that he was going to be worse. His head throbbed; the room seemed turning round with him, and when it settled, he saw strange shapes in it. A few rays of the sinking moon had got in between the curtains of one of the windows, and had waked up everything! The furniture looked odd—unpleasantly odd. Something unnatural, or at least unearthly, must be near him! The room was an old-fashioned one, in thorough keeping with the age of the house—the very haunt for a ghost, but he had heard of no ghost in that room! He got up to get himself some water, and drew the curtains aside. He could have been in no thraldom to an apprehensive imagination; for what man, with a brooding terror couched in him, would, in the middle of the night, let in the moon? To such a passion, she is worse than the deepest darkness, especially when going down, as she was then, with the weary look she gets by the time her work is about over, and she has long been forsaken of the poor mortals for whom she has so often to be up and shining all night. He poured himself some water and drank it, but thought it did not taste nice. Then he turned to the window, and looked out.

The house was in a large park. Its few trees served mainly to show how wide the unbroken spaces of grass. Before the house, motionless as a statue, stood a great gray horse with hanging neck, his shadow stretched in mighty grotesque behind him, and on his back the very effigy of my uncle, motionless too as marble. The horse stood sidewise to the house, but the face of his rider was turned toward it, as if scanning its windows in the dying glitter of the moon. John thought he heard a cry somewhere, and went to his door, but, listening hard, heard nothing. When he looked again from the window, the apparition seemed fainter, and farther away, though neither horse nor rider had changed posture. He rubbed his eyes to see more plainly, could no longer distinguish the appearance, and went back to bed. In the morning he was in a high fever—unconscious save of restless discomfort and undefined trouble.

He learned afterward from the housekeeper, that his mother herself nursed him, but he would take neither food nor medicine from her hand. No doctor was sent for. John thought, and I cannot but think, that the water in his bottle had to do with the sudden illness. His mother may have merely wished to prevent him from coming to me; but, for the time at least, the conviction had got possession of him, that she was attempting his life. He may have argued in semi-conscious moments, that she would not scruple to take again what she was capable of imagining she had given. Her attentions, however, may have arisen from alarm at seeing him worse than she had intended to make him, and desire to counteract what she had done.

For several days he was prostrate with extreme exhaustion. Necessarily, I knew nothing of this; neither was I, notwithstanding my more than doubt of his mother, in any immediate dread of what she might do. The cessation of his visits could, of course, cause me no anxiety, seeing it was thoroughly understood between us that we were not at liberty to meet.

CHAPTER 20

A Strange Visit

ON the fifth night after that on which he left me to walk home, I was roused, about two o'clock, by a sharp sound as of sudden hail against my window, ceasing as soon as it began. Wondering what it was, for hail it could hardly be, I sprang from the bed, pulled aside the curtain, and looked out. There was light enough in the moon to show me a man looking up at the window, and love enough in my heart to tell me who he was. How he knew the window mine, I have always forgotten to ask him. I would have drawn back, for it vexed me sorely to think him too weak to hold to our agreement, but the face I looked down upon was so ghastly and deathlike, that I perceived at once his coming must have its justification. I did not speak, for I would not have any in the house hear; but, putting on my shoes and a big cloak, I went softly down the stair, opened the door noiselessly, and ran to the other side of the house. There stood John, with his eyes fixed on my window. As I turned the corner I could see, by their weary flashing, that either something terrible had happened, or he was very ill. He stood motionless, unaware of my approach.

"What is it?" I said under my breath, putting a hand on his shoulder.

He did not turn his head or answer me, but grew yet whiter, gasped, and seemed ready to fall. I put my arm round him, and his head sank on the top of mine.

Whatever might be the matter, the first thing was to get him into the house, and make him lie down. I moved a little, holding him fast, and mechanically he followed his support; so that, although with some difficulty, I soon got him round the house, and into the great hall-kitchen, our usual sitting-room; there was fire there that would only want rousing, and, warm as was the night, I felt him very cold. I let him sink on the wide sofa, covered him with my cloak, and ran to rouse old Penny. The aged sleep lightly, and she was up in an instant. I told her that a gentleman I knew had come to the house, either sleep-walking or delirious, and she must come and help me with him. She struck a light, and followed me to the kitchen.

John lay with his eyes closed, in a dead faint. We got him to swallow some brandy, and presently he came to himself a little. Then we put him in my warm bed, and covered him with blankets. In a minute or so he was fast asleep. He had not spoken a word. I left Penny to watch him, and went and dressed myself, thinking hard. The result was, that, having enjoined Penny to let no one near him, *whoever* it might be, I went to the stable, saddled Zoe, and set off for Wittenage.

It was sixteen miles of a ride. The moon went down, and the last of my journey was very dark, for the night was cloudy; but we arrived in safety, just as the dawn was promising to come as soon as it could. No one in the town seemed up, or thinking of getting up. I had learned a lesson from John, however, and I knew Martha's window, which happily looked on the street. I got off Zoe, who was tired enough to stand still, for she was getting old and I had not spared her, and proceeded to search for a stone small enough to throw at the window. The scared face of Martha showed itself almost immediately.

"It's me!" I cried, no louder than she could just hear; "it's me, Martha! Come down and let me in."

Without a word of reply, she left the window, and after some fumbling with the lock, opened the door, and came out to me, looking gray with scare, but none the less with all her wits to her hand.

"How is my uncle, Martha?" I said.

"Much better," she answered.

"Then I must see him at once!"

"He's fast asleep, child! It would be a world's pity to wake him!"

"It would be a worse pity not!" I returned.

"Very well: must-be must!" she answered.

I made Zoe fast to the lamp-post: the night was warm, and hot as she was, she would take no hurt. Then I followed Martha up the stair.

But my uncle was awake. He had heard a little of our motions and whisperings, and lay in expectation of something.

"I thought I should hear from you soon!" he said. "I wrote to Mr. Day on Thursday, but have had no reply. What has happened? Nothing serious, I hope?"

"I hardly know, uncle. John Day is lying at our house, unable to move or speak."

My uncle started up as if to spring from his bed, but fell back again with a groan.

"Don't be alarmed, uncle!" I said. "He is, I hope, safe for the moment, with Penny to watch him; but I am very anxious Dr. Southwell should see him."

"How did it come about, little one?"

"There has been no accident that I know of. But I scarcely know more than you," I replied—and told him all that had taken place within my ken.

He lay silent a moment, thinking.

"I can't say I like his lying there with only Penny to protect him!" he said. "He must have come seeking refuge! I don't like the thing at all! He is in some danger we do not know!"

"I will go back at once, uncle," I replied, and rose from the bedside, where I had seated myself a little tired.

"You must, if we cannot do better. But I think we can. Martha shall go, and you will stay with me. Run at once and wake Dr. Southwell. Ask him to come directly."

I ran all the way—it was not far—and pulled the doctor's night-bell. He answered it himself. I gave him my uncle's message, and he was at the inn a few minutes after me. My uncle told him what had happened, and begged him to go and see the patient, carrying Martha with him in his gig.

The doctor said he would start at once. My uncle begged him to give strictest orders that *no* one was to see Mr. Day, whoever it might be. Martha heard, and grew like a colonel of dragoons ordered to charge with his regiment.

In less than half an hour they started—at a pace that delighted me.

When Zoe was put up and attended to, and I was alone with my uncle, I got him some breakfast to make up for the loss of his sleep. He told me it was better than sleep to have me near him.

What I went through that night and the following day, I need not recount. Whoever has loved one in danger and out of her reach, will know what it was like. The doctor did not make his appearance until five o'clock, having seen several patients on his way back. The young man, he reported, was certainly in for a fever of some kind—he could not yet pronounce which. He would see him again on the morrow, he said, and by that time it would have declared itself. Some one in the neighbour-hood must watch the case; it was impossible for him to give it sufficient attention. My uncle told him he was now quite equal to the task himself, and we would all go together the next day. My delight at the proposal was almost equalled by my satisfaction that the doctor made no objection to it.

For joy I scarcely slept that night: I was going to nurse John! But I was anxious about my uncle. He assured me, however, that in one day more he would in any case have insisted on returning. If it had not been for a little lingering fever, he said, he would have gone much sooner.

"That was because of me, uncle!" I answered with contrition.

"Perhaps," he replied; "but I had a blow on the head, you know!"

"There is one good thing," I said: "you will know John

the sooner from seeing him ill! But perhaps you will count that only a mood, uncle, and not to be trusted!"

He smiled. I think he was not *very* anxious about the result of a nearer acquaintance with John Day. I believe he had some faith in my spiritual instinct.

Uncle went with the doctor in his brougham, and I rode Zoe. The back of the house came first in sight, and I saw the window-blinds of my room still down. The doctor had pronounced it the fittest for the invalid, and would not have him moved to the guest-chamber Penny had prepared for him.

In the only room I had ever occupied as my own, I nursed John for a space of three weeks.

From the moment he saw me, he began to improve. My uncle noted this, and I fancy liked John the better for it. Nor did he fail to note the gentleness and gratitude of the invalid.

CHAPTER 21

A Foiled Attempt

❦

THE morning after my uncle's return, came a messenger from Rising with his lady's compliments, asking if
Mr. Whichcote could tell her anything of her son: he had
left the house unseen, during a feverish attack, and as she
could get no tidings of him, she was in great anxiety. She
had accidentally heard that he had made Mr. Whichcote's acquaintance, and therefore took the liberty of
extending to him the inquiry she had already made
everywhere else among his friends. My uncle wrote in
answer, that her son had come to his house in a high
fever; that he had been under medical care ever since;
and that he hoped in a day or two he might be able to
return. If he expressed a desire to see his mother, he
would immediately let her know, but in the meantime it
was imperative he should be kept quiet.

From this letter, Lady Cairnedge might surmise that

her relations with her son were at least suspected. Within two hours came another message—that she would send a close carriage to bring him home the next day. Then indeed were my uncle and I glad that we had come. For though Martha would certainly have defended the citadel to her utmost, she might have been sorely put to it if his mother proceeded to carry him away by force. My uncle, in reply, begged her not to give herself the useless trouble of sending to fetch him: in the state he was in at present, it would be tantamount to murder to remove him, and he would not be a party to it.

When I yielded my place in the sick-room to Martha and went to bed, my heart was not only at ease for the night, but I feared nothing for the next day with my uncle on my side—or rather on John's side.

We were just rising from our early dinner, for we were old-fashioned people, when up drove a grand carriage, with two strong footmen behind, and a servant in plain clothes on the box by the coachman. It pulled up at the door, and the man on the box got down and rang the bell, while his fellows behind got down also, and stood together a little way behind him. My uncle at once went to the hall, but no more than in time, for there was Penny already on her way to open the door. He opened it himself, and stood on the threshold.

"If you please, sir," said the man, not without arrogance, "we're come to take Mr. Day home."

"Tell your mistress," returned my uncle, "that Mr. Day has expressed no desire to return, and is much too unwell to be informed of her ladyship's wish."

"Begging your pardon, sir," said the man, "we have her ladyship's orders to bring him. We'll take every possible care of him. The carriage is an extra-easy one, and I'll sit inside with the young gentleman myself. If he ain't right in his head, he'll never know nothink till he comes to himself in his own bed."

My uncle had let the man talk, but his anger was fast rising.

"I cannot let him go. I would not send a beggar to the hospital in the state he is in."

"But, indeed, sir, you must! We have our orders."

"If you fancy I will dismiss a guest of mine at the order of any human being, were it the queen's own majesty," said my uncle—I heard the words, and with my mind's eyes saw the blue flash of his as he said them—"you will find yourself mistaken."

"I'm sorry," said the man quietly, "but I have my orders! Let me pass, please. It is my business to find the young gentleman, and take him home. No one can have the right to keep him against his mother's will, especially when he's not in a fit state to judge for himself."

"Happily I am in a fit state to judge for him," said my uncle, coldly.

"I dare not go back without him. Let me pass," he returned, raising his voice a little, and approaching the door as if he would force his way.

I ought to have mentioned that, as my uncle went to the door, he took from a rack in the hall a whip with a bamboo stock, which he generally carried when he rode. His answer to the man was a smart, though left-handed blow with the stock across his face: they were too near for the thong. He staggered back, and stood holding his hand to his face. His fellow-servants, who, during the colloquy, had looked on with gentlemanlike imperturba-

bility, made a simultaneous step forward. My uncle sent
the thong with a hiss about their ears. They sprang toward him in a fury, but halted immediately and recoiled.
He had drawn a small swordlike weapon, which I did not
know to be there, from the stock of the whip. He gave
one swift glance behind him. I was in the hall at his back.

"Shut the door, Orba," he cried.

I shut him out, and ran to a window in the little drawing-room, which commanded the door. Never had I seen
him look as now—his pale face pale no longer, but
flushed with anger. Neither, indeed, until that moment
had I ever seen the *natural* look of anger, the expression
of *pure* anger. There was nothing mean or ugly in it—not
an atom of hate. But how his eyes blazed!

"Go back," he cried, in a voice far more stern than
loud. "If one of you set foot on the lowest step, and I will
run him through."

The men saw he meant it; they saw the closed door,
and my uncle with his back to it. They turned and spoke
to each other. The coachman sat immovable on his box.
They mounted, and he drove away.

I ran and opened the door. My uncle came in with a
smile. He went up the stair, and I followed him to the
room where the invalid lay. We were both anxious to
learn if he had been disturbed.

He was leaning on his elbow, listening. He looked a
good deal more like himself.

"I knew you would defend me, sir!" he said, with a
respectful confidence which could not but please my
uncle.

"You did not want to go home—did you?" he asked
with a smile.

"I should have thrown myself out of the carriage!" answered John; "—that is, if they had got me into it. But, please, tell me, sir," he went on, "how it is I find myself in your house? I have been puzzling over it all the morning. I have no recollection of coming."

"You understand, I fancy," rejoined my uncle, "that one of the family has a notion she can take better care of you than anybody else! Is not that enough to account for it?"

"Hardly, sir. Belorba cannot have gone and rescued me from my mother!"

"How do you know that? Belorba is a terrible creature when she is roused. But you have talked enough. Shut your eyes, and don't trouble yourself to recollect. As you get stronger, it will all come back to you. Then you will be able to tell us, instead of asking us to tell you."

He left us together. I quieted John by reading to him, and absolutely declining to talk.

"You are a captive. The castle is enchanted: speak a single word," I said, "and you will find yourself in the dungeon of your own room."

He looked at me an instant, closed his eyes, and in a few minutes was fast asleep. He slept for two hours, and when he woke was quite himself. He was very weak, but the fever was gone, and we had now only to feed him up, and keep him quiet.

CHAPTER 22

John Recalls and Remembers

WHAT a weight was off my heart! It seemed as if nothing more could go wrong. But, though John was plainly happy, he was not quite comfortable: he worried himself with trying to remember how he had come to us. The last thing he could definitely recall before finding himself with us, was his mother looking at him through a night that seemed made of blackness so solid that he marvelled she could move in it. She brought him something to drink, but he fancied it blood, and would not touch it. He remembered now that there was a red tumbler in his room. He could recall nothing after, except a cold wind, and a sense of utter weariness but absolute compulsion: he must keep on and on till he found the gate of heaven, to which he seemed only for ever coming nearer. His conclusion was, that he knew what he was about every individual moment, but had no memory; each thing he did was immediately forgotten, while the knowledge of what he had to do next remained with him. It was, he thought, a mental condition analogous with walking, in which every step is a frustrated fall. I set this down here, because, when I told my uncle what John had been saying, myself not sure that I perceived what he meant, he declared the boy a philosopher of the finest grain. But he warned me not to encourage his talking, and especially not to ask him to explain. There was nothing, he said, worse for a weak brain, than to set a strong will to work it.

I tried to obey him, but it grew harder as the days went on. There were not many of them, however; he recovered rapidly. When at length my uncle talked not only to but with him, I regarded it as a virtual withdrawal of his prohibition, and after that spoke to John of whatever came into his or my head.

It was then he told me all he could remember since the moment he left me with his supper in his hand. A great part of his recollection was the vision of my uncle on the moor, and afterward in the park. We did not know what to make of it. I should at once have concluded it caused by prelusive illness, but for my remembrance of what both my uncle and myself had seen, so long before, in the thunderstorm; while John, willing enough to attribute its recurrence to that cause, found it impossible to concede that he was anything but well when crossing the moor. I thought, however, that excitement, fatigue, and lack of food, might have something to do with it, and with his illness too; while, if he was in a state to see anything phantasmal, what shape more likely to appear than that of my uncle!

He would not hear of my mentioning the thing to my uncle. I would for my own part have gone to him with it immediately; but could not with John's prayer in my ears. I resolved, however, to gain his consent if I could.

He had by this time as great a respect for my uncle as I had myself, but could not feel at home with him as I did. Whether the vision was only a vision, or indeed my uncle's double, whatever a double may be, the tale of it could hardly be an agreeable one to him; and naturally John shrank from the risk of causing him the least annoyance.

The question of course came up, what he was to do when able to leave us. He had spoken very plainly to my uncle concerning his relations with his mother—had told him indeed that he could not help suspecting he owed his illness to her.

I was nearly always present when they talked, but remember in especial a part of what passed on one occasion.

"I believe I understand my mother," said John, "—but only after much thinking. I loved her when a child; and if she had not left me for the sake of liberty and influence —that at least is how I account for her doing so—I might at this moment be struggling for personal freedom, instead of having that over."

"There are women," returned my uncle, "some of them of the most admired, who are slaves to a demoniacal love of power. The very pleasure of their consciousness consists in the knowledge that they have power— not power to do things, but power to make other people do things. It is an insanity, but a devilishly immoral and hateful insanity.—I do not say the lady in question is one of such, for I do not know her; I only say I have known such a one."

John replied that certainly the love of power was his mother's special weakness. She was spoiled when a child, he had been told; had her every wish regarded, her every whim respected. This ruinous treatment sprang, he said, from the self-same ambition, in another form, on the part of her mother—the longing, namely, to secure her child's supreme affection—with the natural consequence that they came to hate one another. His father and she had been married but fifteen months, when he died of a fall, following the hounds. Within six months she was engaged, but the engagement was broken off, and she went abroad, leaving him behind her. She married lord Cairnedge in Venice, and returned to England when John was nearly four, and seemed to have lost all memory of her. His stepfather was good to him, but died when he was about eight. His mother was very severe. Her object plainly was to plant her authority so in his very nature, that he should never think of disputing her will.

"But," said John, "she killed my love, and so I grew able to cast off her yoke."

"The world would fare worse, I fancy," remarked my uncle, "if violent women bore patient children. The evil would become irremediable. The children might not be ruined, but they would bring no discipline to the mother!"

"Her servants," continued John, "obey her implicitly, except when they are sure she will never know. She treats them so imperiously, that they admire her, and are proud to have such a mistress. But she is convinced at last, I believe, that she will never get me to do as she pleases; and therefore hates me so heartily, that she can hardly keep her ladylike hands off me. I do not think I have been unreasonable; I have not found it difficult to obey others that were set over me; but when I found almost her every requirement part of a system for reducing me to a slavish obedience, I began to lay down lines of my own. I resolved to do at once whatever she asked me, whether pleasant to me or not, so long as I saw no reason why it should not be done. Then I was surprised to find how seldom I had to make a stand against her wishes. At the same time, the mode in which she conveyed her pleasure, was invariably such as to make a pretty strong effort of the will necessary for compliance with it. But the effort to overcome the difficulty caused by her manner, helped to develop in me the strength to resist where it was not right to yield. By far the most serious difference we had yet had, arose about six months ago, when she insisted I should make myself agreeable to a certain lady, whom I by no means disliked. She had planned our marriage, I believe, as one of her parallels in the siege of the lady's noble father, then a widower of a year. I told her I would not lay myself out to please any lady, except I wanted to marry her. 'And why, pray, should you not marry her?' she returned. I answered that I did not love her, and would not marry until I saw the woman I could not be happy without, and she accepted me. She went into a terrible passion, but I found myself quite unmoved by it: it is a wonderful heartener to know yourself not merely standing up for a right, but for the right to do the right thing! 'You wouldn't surely have me marry a woman I didn't care a straw for!' I said. 'Quench my soul!' she cried—I have often wondered where she learned the oath—'what would that matter? She wouldn't care a straw for you in a month!'—'Why should I marry her then?'—'Because your mother wishes it,' she replied, and turned to march from the room as if that settled the thing. But I could not leave it so. The sooner she understood the better! 'Mother!' I cried, 'I will not marry the lady. I will not pay her the least attention that could be mistaken to mean the possibility of it.' She turned upon me. I have just respect enough left for her, not to say what her face suggested to me. She was pale as a corpse; her very lips were colourless; her eyes—but I will not go on. 'Your father all over!' she snarled—yes, snarled, with an inarticulate cry of fiercest loathing, and turned again and went. If I do not quite think my mother, *at present,* would murder me, I do think she would do anything short of murder to gain her ends with me. But do not be afraid; I am sufficiently afraid to be on my guard.

"My father was a rich man, and left my mother more than enough; there was no occasion for her to marry again, except she loved, and I am sure she did not love lord Cairnedge. I wish, for my sake, not for his, he were alive now. But the moment, I am one and twenty, I shall be my own master, and hope, sir, you will not count me unworthy to be the more Belorba's servant. One thing I am determined upon: my mother shall not cross my threshold but at my wife's invitation; and I shall never ask my wife to invite her. She is too dangerous.

"We had another altercation about Miss Miles, an hour or two before I first saw Orba. They were far from worthy feelings that possessed me up to the moment when I caught sight of her over the wall. It was a leap out

of hell into paradise. The glimpse of such a face, without
shadow of scheme or plan or selfish end, was salvation
to me. I thank God!"

Perhaps I ought not to let those words about myself
stand, but he said them.

He had talked too long. He fell back in his chair, and
the tears began to gather in his eyes. My uncle rose, put
his arm about me, and led me to the study.

"Let him rest a bit, little one," he said as we entered.
"It is long since we had a good talk!"

He seated himself in his think-chair—a name which,
when a child, I had given it, and I slid to the floor at his
feet.

"I cannot help thinking, little one," he began, "that
you are going to be a happy woman! I do believe that is
a man to be trusted. As for the mother, there is no occasion to think of her, beyond being on your guard against
her. You will have no trouble with her after you are
married."

"I cannot help fearing she will do us a mischief,
uncle," I returned.

"Sir Philip Sidney says—'Since a man is bound no
further to himself than to do wisely, chance is only to
trouble them that stand upon chance.' That is, we are
responsible only for our actions, not for their results.
Trust first in God, then in John Day."

"I was sure you would like him, uncle!" I cried, with
a flutter of loving triumph.

"I was nearly as sure myself—such confidence had I in
the instinct of my little one. I think that I, of the two of
us, may, in this instance, claim the greater faith!"

"You are always before me, uncle!" I said. "I only

follow where you lead. But what do you think the woman will do next?"

"I don't think. It is no use. We shall hear of her before long. If all mothers were like her, the world would hardly be saved!"

"It would not be worth saving, uncle."

"Whatever can be saved, must be worth saving, my child."

"Yes, uncle; I shouldn't have said that," I replied.

CHAPTER 23

Letter and Answer

W<small>E</small> did hear of her before long. The next morning a letter was handed to my uncle as we sat at breakfast. He looked hard at the address, changed countenance, and frowned very dark, but I could not read the frown. Then his face cleared a little; he opened, read, and handed the letter to me.

Lady Cairnedge hoped Mr. Whichcote would excuse one who had so lately come to the neighbourhood, that, until an hour ago, she knew nothing of the position and character of the gentleman in whose house her son had, in a momentary, but, alas! not unusual aberration, sought shelter, and found generous hospitality. She apologized heartily for the unceremonious way in which she had sent for him. In her anxiety to have him home, if possible, before he should realize his awkward position in the house of a stranger, she had been inconsiderate!

She left it to the judgment of his kind host whether she should herself come to fetch him, or send her carriage with the medical man who usually attended him. In either case her servants must accompany the carriage, as he would probably object to being removed. He might, however, be perfectly manageable, for he was, when himself, the gentlest creature in the world!

I was in a rage. I looked up, expecting to see my uncle as indignant with the diabolical woman as I was myself. But he seemed sunk in reverie, his body present, his spirit far away. A pang shot through my heart. Could the wicked device have told already?

"May I ask, uncle," I said, and tried hard to keep my voice steady, "how you mean to answer this vile epistle?"

He looked up with a wan smile, such as might have broke from Lazarus when he found himself again in his body.

"I will take it to the young man," he answered.

"Please, let us go at once then, uncle! I cannot sit still."

He rose, and we went together to John's room.

He was much better—sitting up in bed, and eating the breakfast Penny had carried him.

"I have just had a letter from your mother, Day," said my uncle.

"Indeed!" returned John dryly.

"Will you read it, and tell me what answer you would like me to return."

"Hardly like her usual writing—though there's her own strange S!" remarked John as he looked at it.

"Does she always make an S like that?" asked my uncle, with something peculiar in his tone, I thought.

"None, my darling," he answered. "The thing that made me talk to you so against secrets when you were a child, was, that I had one myself—one that was, and is, eating the heart out of me. But that woman shall not know and you be ignorant! I will not have a secret with *her!*—Leave me now, please, little one."

I rose at once.

"May I take the letter with me, uncle?" I asked.

He rubbed his forehead with a still trembling hand. The trembling of that beloved hand filled me with such a divine sense of pity that for the first time I seemed to know God, causing in me that consciousness! The whole human mother was roused in me for my uncle. I would die, I would kill to save him! The worm was welcome to swallow me! My very being was a well of loving pity, pouring itself out over that trembling hand.

He took up the letter, gave it to me, and turned his face away with a groan. I left the room in strange exaltation —the exaltation of merest love.

I went to the study, and there read the hateful letter. Here it is. Having transcribed it, I shall destroy it.

"Sir,—For one who persists in coming between a woman and her son, who will blame the mother if she cast aside forbearance! I would have spared you as hith-erto; I will spare you no longer. You little thought when you crossed me who I was—the one in the world in whose power you lay! I would perish everlastingly rather than permit one of my blood to marry one of yours. My words are strong; you are welcome to call them unlady-like; but you shall not doubt what I mean. You know perfectly that, if I denounce you as a murderer, I can

"Always—like a snake just going to strike."

My uncle's face grew ghastly pale. He almost snatched the letter from John's hand, looked at it, gave it back to him, and, to our dismay, left the room.

"What can be the matter, John?" I said, my heart sinking within me.

"Go to him," said John.

I dared not. I had often seen him *like* that before walking out into the night; but there was something in his face now which I had not seen there before. It looked as if some terrible suspicion were suddenly confirmed.

"You see what my mother is after!" said John. "You have now to believe *her,* that I am subject to fits of insanity, or to believe *me,* that there is nothing she will not do to get her way."

"Her object is clear," I replied. "But if she thinks to fool my uncle, she will find herself mistaken!"

"She hopes to fool both you and your uncle," he rejoined. "The only wise thing I could do, she will handle so as to convince any expert of my madness—I mean, my coming to you! My reasons will go for nothing—less than nothing—with any one she chooses to bewitch. She will look at me with an anxious love no doctor could doubt. No one can know—*you* do not know that I am not mad —or at least subject to attacks of madness!"

"Oh, John, don't frighten me!" I cried.

"There! you are not sure about it!"

It seemed cruel of him to tease me so; but I saw presently why he did it: he thought his mother's letter had waked a doubt in my uncle; and he wanted me not to be vexed with my uncle, even if he deserted him and went over to his mother's side.

"I love your uncle," he said. "I know he is a true man! I *will* not be angry with him if my mother do mislead him. The time will come when he will know the truth. It must appear at last! I shall have to fight her alone, that's all! The worst is, if he thinks with my mother I shall have to go at once!—If only somebody would sell my horse for me!"

I guessed that his mother kept him short of money, and remembered with gladness that I was not quite penniless at the moment.

"In the meantime, you must keep as quiet as you can, John," I said. "Where is the good of planning upon an *if*? To trust is to get ready, uncle says. Trust is better than foresight."

John required little such persuading. And indeed something very different was in my uncle's mind from what John feared.

Presently I caught a glimpse of him riding out of the yard. I ran to a window from which I could see the edge of the moor, and saw him cross it at an uphill gallop.

He was gone about four hours, and on his return went straight to his own room. Not until nine o'clock did I go to him, and then he came with me to supper.

He looked worn, but was kind and genial as usual. After supper he sent for Dick, and told him to ride to Rising, the first thing in the morning, with a letter he would find on the hall-table.

The letter he read to us before we parted for the night. It was all we could have wished. He wrote that he must not have any one in his house interfered with; so long as a man was his guest, he was his servant. Her ladyship had, however, a perfect right to see her son, and would be welcome; only the decision as to his going or remaining must rest with the young man himself. If he chose to accompany his mother, well and good! though he should be sorry to lose him. If he declined to return with her, he and his house continued at his service.

CHAPTER 24

Hand to Hand

WE looked for Lady Cairnedge all the next day. John was up by noon, and ready to receive her in the drawing-room; he would not see her in his bedroom. But the hours passed, and she did not come.

In the evening, however, when the twilight was thickening, and already all was dark in the alleys of the garden, her carriage drove quietly up—with a startling scramble of arrest at the door. The same servants were outside, and a very handsome dame within. As she descended, I saw that she was tall, and, if rather stout, not stouter than suited her age and style. Her face was pale, but she seemed in perfect health. When I saw her closer, I found her features the most regular I had ever seen. Had the soul within it filled the mould of that face, it would have been beautiful. As it was, it was only handsome—to me repulsive. The moment I saw it, I knew myself in the presence of a masked battery.

My uncle had insisted that she should be received where we usually sat, and had given Penny orders to show her into the hall-kitchen.

I was alone there, preparing something for John. We were not expecting her, for it seemed now too late to look for her. My uncle was in the study, and Martha somewhere about the house. My heart sank as I turned from the window, and sank yet lower when she appeared in the doorway of the kitchen. But as I advanced, I caught sight of my uncle, and went boldly to meet the enemy. He had come down his stair, and had just stepped into a clear blaze of light, which that moment burst from the wood I had some time ago laid damp upon the fire. The next instant I saw the lady's countenance ghastly with terror, looking beyond me. I turned, but saw nothing, save that my uncle had disappeared. When I faced her again, only a shadow of her fright remained. I offered her my hand—for she was John's mother, but she did not take it. She stood scanning me from head to foot.

"I am Lady Cairnedge," she said. "Where is my son?"

I turned yet again. My uncle had not come back. I was not prepared to take his part. I was bewildered. A dead silence fell. For the first time in my life, my uncle seemed to have deserted me, and at the moment when most I needed him! I turned once more to the lady, and said, hardly knowing what,

"You wish to see Mr. Day?"

She answered me with a cold stare.

"I will go and tell him you are here," I faltered; and passing her, I sped along the passage to the drawing-room.

"John!" I cried, bursting in, "she's come! Do you still mean to see her? Are you able? Uncle——"

There I stopped, for his eyes were stern, and not looking at me, but at something behind me. One moment I thought his fever had returned, but following his gaze I looked round:—there stood Lady Cairnedge! John was face to face with his mother, and my uncle was not there to defend him!

"Are you ready?" she said, nor pretended greeting. She seemed slightly discomposed, and in haste.

I was by this time well aware of my lover's determination of character, but I was not prepared for the tone in which he addressed the icy woman calling herself his mother.

"I am ready to listen," he answered.

"John!" she returned, with mingled severity and sharpness, "let us have no masquerading! You are perfectly fit to come home, and you must come at once. The carriage is at the door."

"You are quite right, mother," answered John calmly; "I *am* fit to go home with you. But Rising does not quite agree with me. I dread such another attack, and do not mean to go."

The drawing-room had a rectangular bay-window, one of whose three sides commanded the door. The opposite side looked into a little grove of larches. Lady Cairnedge had already realized the position of the room. She darted to the window, and saw her carriage but a few yards away.

She would have thrown up the sash, but found she could not. She twisted her handkerchief round her gloved hand, and dashed it through a pane.

"Men!" she cried, in a loud, commanding voice, "come at once."

The moment she went to the window, I sprang to the door, locked it, put the key in my pocket, and set my back to the door.

I heard the men thundering at the hall-door. Lady Cairnedge turned as if she would herself go and open to them, but seeing me, she understood what I had done, and went back to the window.

"Come here! Come to me here—to the window!" she cried.

John had been watching with a calm, determined look. He came and stood between us.

"John," I said, "leave your mother to me."

"She will kill you!" he answered.

"You might kill her!" I replied.

I darted to the chimney, where a clear fire was burning, caught up the poker, and thrust it between the bars.

"That's for you!" I whispered. "They will not touch you with that in your hand! Never mind me. If your mother move hand or foot to help them, it will be my turn!"

He gave me a smile and a nod, and his eyes lightened. I saw that he trusted me, and I felt fearless as a bull-dog.

In the meantime, she had spoken to her servants, and was now trying to open the window, which had a peculiar catch. I saw that John could defend himself much better at the window than in the room. I went softly behind his mother, put my hands round her neck, and clasping them in front, pulled her backward with all my strength. We fell on the floor together, I under of course, but clutching as if all my soul were in my fingers. Neither should she meddle with John, nor should he lay hand on her! I did not mind much what I did to her myself.

"To the window, John," I cried, "and break their heads!"

He snatched the poker from the fire, and the next moment I heard a crashing of glass, but of course I could not see what was going on. Mine was no grand way of fighting, but what was dignity where John was in danger! For the moment I had the advantage, but, while determined to hold on to the last, I feared she would get the better of me, for she was much bigger and stronger, and crushed and kicked, and dug her elbows into me, struggling like a mad woman.

All at once the tug of her hands on mine ceased. She gave a great shriek, and I felt a shudder go through her. Then she lay still. I relaxed my hold cautiously, for I feared a trick. She did not move. Horror seized me; I thought I had killed her. I writhed from under her to see. As I did so, I caught sight of the pale face of my uncle, looking in at that part of the window next the larch-grove. Immediately I remembered lady Cairnedge's terror in the kitchen, and knew that the cause of it, and of her present cry, must be the same, to wit, the sight of my uncle. I had not hurt her! I was not yet on my feet when my uncle left the window, flew to the other side of it, and fell upon the men with a stick so furiously that he drove them to the carriage. The horses took fright, and went prancing about, rearing and jibbing. At the call of the coachman, two of the men flew to their heads. I saw no more of their assailant.

John, who had not got a fair blow at one of his besiegers, left the window, and came to me where I was trying to restore his mother. The third man, the butler, came back to the window, put his hand through, undid the catch, and flung the sash wide. John caught up the poker from the floor, and darted to it.

"Set foot within the window, Parker," he cried, "and I will break your head."

The man did not believe he would hurt him, and put foot and head through the window.

Now John had honestly threatened, but to perform he found harder than he had thought: it is one thing to raise a poker, and another to strike a head with it. The window was narrow, and the whole man was not yet in the room, when John raised his weapon; but he could not bring the horrid poker down upon the dumb blind back of the stooping man's head. He threw it from him, and casting his eyes about, spied a huge family-bible on a side-table. He sprang to it, and caught it up—just in time. The man had got one foot firm on the floor, and was slowly drawing in the other, when down came the bible on his head, with all the force John could add to its weight. The butler tumbled senseless on the floor.

"Here, Orbie!" cried John; "help me to bundle him out before he comes to himself.—Take what you would have!" he said, as between us we shoved him out on the gravel.

I fetched smelling-salts and brandy, and everything I could think of—fetched Martha too, and between us we got her on the sofa, but Lady Cairnedge lay motionless. She breathed indeed, but did not open her eyes. John stood ready to do anything for her, but his countenance revealed little compassion. Whatever the cause of his mother's swoon—he had never seen her in one before—

he was certain it had to do with some bad passage in her life. He said so to me that same evening. "But what could the sight of my uncle have to do with it?" I asked. "Probably he knows something, or she thinks he does," he answered.

"Wouldn't it be better to put her to bed, and send for the doctor, John?" I suggested at last.

Perhaps the sound of my voice calling her son by his Christian name, stung her proud ear, for the same moment she sat up, passed her hands over her eyes, and cast a scared gaze about the room.

"Where am I? Is it gone?" she murmured, looking ghastly.

No one answered her.

"Call Parker," she said, feebly, yet imperiously.

Still no one spoke.

She kept glancing sideways at the window, where nothing was to be seen but the gathering night. In a few moments she rose and walked straight from the room, erect, but white as a corpse. I followed, passed her, and opened the hall-door. There stood the carriage, waiting, as if nothing unusual had happened, Parker seated in the rumble, with one of the footmen beside him. The other man stood by the carriage-door. He opened it immediately; her ladyship stepped in, and dropped on the seat; the carriage rolled away.

I went back to John.

"I must leave you, darling!" he said. "I cannot subject you to the risk of such another outrage! I fear sometimes my mother may be what she would have you think me. I ought to have said, I hope she is. It would be the only possible excuse for her behaviour. The natural end of loving one's own way, is to go mad. If you don't get it, you go mad; if you do get it, you go madder—that's all the difference!—I must go!"

I tried to expostulate with him, but it was of no use.

"Where will you go?" I said. "You cannot go home!"

"I would at once," he answered, "if I could take the reins in my own hands. But I will go to London, and see the family-lawyer. He will tell me what I had better do."

"You have no money!" I said.

"How do you know that?" he returned with a smile. "Have you been searching my pockets?"

"John!" I cried.

He broke into a merry laugh.

"Your uncle will lend me a five-pound-note," he said.

"He will lend you as much as you want; but I don't think he's in the house," I answered. "I have two myself, though! I'll run and fetch them."

I bounded away to get the notes. It was like having a common purse already, to lend John ten pounds! But I had no intention of letting him leave the house the same day he was first out of his room after such an illness—that was, if I could help it.

My uncle had given me the use of a drawer in that same cabinet in which were the precious stones; and there, partly, I think, from the pride of sharing the cabinet with my uncle, I had long kept everything I counted precious: I should have kept Zoe there if she had not been alive and too big!

CHAPTER 25

A Very Strange Thing

THE moment I opened the door of the study, I saw my uncle—in his think-chair, his head against the back of it, his face turned to the ceiling. I ran to his side and dropped on my knees, thinking he was dead. He opened his eyes and looked at me, but with such a wan, woe-begone countenance, that I burst into a passion of tears.

"What is it, uncle dear?" I gasped and sobbed.

"Nothing very new, little one," he answered.

"It is something terrible, uncle," I cried, "or you would not look like that! Did those horrid men hurt you? You did give it them well! You came down on them like the angel on the Assyrians!"

"I don't know what you're talking about, little one!" he returned. "What men?"

"The men that came with John's mother to carry him off. If it hadn't been for my beautiful uncle, they would have done it too! How I wondered what had become of you! I was almost in despair. I thought you had left us to ourselves—and you only waiting, like God, for the right moment!"

He sat up, and stared at me, bewildered.

"I had forgotten all about John!" he said. "As to what you think I did, I know nothing about it. I haven't been out of this room since I saw—that spectre in the kitchen."

"John's mother, you mean, uncle?"

"Ah! she's John's mother, is she? Yes, I thought as much—and it was more than my poor brain could stand! It was too terrible!—My little one, this is death to you and me!"

My heart sank within me. One thought only went through my head—that, come what might, I would no more give up John, than if I were already married to him in the church.

"But why—what is it, uncle?" I said, hardly able to get the words out.

"I will tell you another time," he answered, and rising, went to the door.

"John is going to London," I said, following him.

"Is he?" he returned listlessly.

"He wants to see his lawyer, and try to get things on a footing of some sort between his mother and him."

"That is very proper," he replied, with his hand on the lock.

"But you don't think it would be safe for him to travel to-night—do you, uncle—so soon after his illness?" I asked.

"No, I cannot say I do. It would not be safe. He is welcome to stop till to-morrow."

"Will you not tell him so, uncle? He is bent on going!"

"I would rather not see him! There is no occasion. It will be a great relief to me when he is able—quite able, I mean—to go home to his mother—or where it may suit him best."

It was indeed like death to hear my uncle talk so differently about John. What had he done to be treated in this way—taken up and made a friend of, and then cast off without reason given! My dear uncle was not at all like himself! To say he forgot our trouble and danger, and never came near us in our sore peril, when we owed our deliverance to him! and now to speak like this concerning John! Something was terribly wrong with him! I dared hardly think what it could be.

I stood speechless.

My uncle opened the door, and went down the steps. The sound of his feet along the corridor and down the stair to the kitchen, died away in my ears. My life seemed to go ebbing with it. I was stranded on a desert shore, and he in whom I had trusted was leaving me there!

I came to myself a little, got the two five-pound-notes, and returned to John.

When I reached the door of the room, I found my heart in my throat, and my brains upside down. What was I to say to him? How could I let him go away so late? and how could I let him stay where his departure would be a relief? Even I would have him gone from where he was not wanted! I saw, however, that my uncle must not have John's death at his door—that I must persuade him to stay the night. I went in, and gave him the notes, but begged him, for my love, to go to bed. In the morning, I said, I would drive him to the station.

He yielded with difficulty—but with how little suspicion that all the time I wished him gone! I went to bed only to lie listening for my uncle's return. It was long past midnight ere he came.

In the morning I sent Penny to order the phaeton, and then ran to my uncle's room, in the hope he would want to see John before he left: I was not sure he had realized that he was going.

He was neither in, his bed-room nor in the study. I went to the stable. Dick was putting the horse to the phaeton. He told me he had heard his master, two hours before, saddle Thanatos, and ride away. This made me yet more anxious about him. He did not often ride out early—seldom indeed after coming home late! Things seemed to threaten complication!

John looked so much better, and was so eager after the projected interview with his lawyer, that I felt comforted concerning him. I did not tell him what my uncle had said the night before. It would, I felt, be wrong to mention what my uncle might wish forgotten; and as I did not know what he meant, it could serve no end. We parted at the station very much as if we had been married half a century, and I returned home to brood over the strange things that had happened. But before long I found myself in a weltering swamp of futile speculation, and turned my thoughts perforce into other channels, lest I should lose the power of thinking, and be drowned in reverie: my uncle had taught me that reverie is Phaeton in the chariot of Apollo.

The weary hours passed, and my uncle did not come. I had never before been really uneasy at his longest absence; but now I was far more anxious about him than about John. Alas, through me fresh trouble had befallen my uncle as well as John! When the night came, I went to bed, for I was very tired: I must keep myself strong, for something unfriendly was on its way, and I must be able to meet it! I knew well I should not sleep until I heard the sounds of his arrival: those came about one o'clock, and in a moment I was dreaming.

In my dream I was still awake, and still watching for my uncle's return. I heard the sound of Death's hoofs, not on the stones of the yard, but on the gravel before the house, and coming round the house till under my window. There he stopped, and I heard my uncle call to me to come down: he wanted me. In my dream I was a child; I sprang out of bed, ran from the house on my bare feet, jumped into his down-stretched arms, and was in a moment seated in front of him. Death gave a great plunge, and went off like the wind, cleared the gate in a flying stride, and rushed up the hill to the heath. The wind was blowing behind us furiously: I could hear it roaring, but did not feel it, for it could not overtake us; we outstripped and kept ahead of it; if for a moment we slackened speed, it fell upon us raging.

We came at length to the pool near the heart of the heath, and I wondered that, at the speed we were making, we had been such a time in reaching it. It was the dismalest spot, with its crumbling peaty banks, and its water brown as tea. Tradition declared it had no bottom —went down into nowhere.

"Here," said my uncle, bringing his horse to a sudden

halt, "we had a terrible battle once, Death and I, with the worm that lives in this hole. You know what worm it is, do you not?"

I had heard of the worm, and any time I happened, in galloping about the heath, to find myself near the pool, the thought would always come back with a fresh shudder—what if the legend were a true one, and the worm was down there biding his time! but anything more about the worm I had never heard.

"No, uncle," I answered; "I don't know what worm it is."

"Ah," he answered, with a sigh, "if you do not take the more care, little one, you will some day learn, not what the worm is called, but what it is! The worm that lives there, is the worm that never dies."

I gave a shriek; I had never heard of the horrible creature before—so it seemed in my dream. To think of its being so near us, and never dying, was too terrible.

"Don't be frightened, little one," he said, pressing me closer to his bosom. "Death and I killed it. Come with me to the other side, and you will see it lying there, stiff and stark."

"But, uncle," I said, "how can it be dead—how can you have killed it, if it never dies?"

"Ah, that is the mystery!" he returned. "But come and see. It was a terrible fight. I never had such a fight—or dear old Death either. But she's dead now! It was worth living for, to make away with such a monster!"

We rode round the pool, cautiously because of the crumbling banks, to see the worm lie dead. On and on we rode. I began to think we must have ridden many times round the hole.

"I wonder where it can be, uncle!" I said at length.

"We shall come to it very soon," he answered.

"But," I said, "mayn't we have ridden past it without seeing it?"

He laughed a loud and terrible laugh.

"When once you have seen it, little one," he replied, "you too will laugh at the notion of having ridden past it without seeing it. The worm that never dies is hardly a thing to escape notice!"

We rode on and on. All at once my uncle threw up his hands, dropping the reins, and with a fearful cry covered his face.

"It is gone! I have not killed it! No, I have *not!* It is here! it is here!" he cried, pressing his hand to his heart. "It is here, and it *was* here all the time I thought it dead! What will become of me! I am lost, lost!"

At the word, old Death gave a scream, and laying himself out, flew with all the might of his swift limbs to get away from the place. But the wind, which was behind us as we came, now stormed in our faces; and presently I saw we should never reach home, for, with all Death's fierce endeavour, we moved but an inch or two in the minute, and that with a killing struggle.

"Little one," said my uncle, "if you don't get down we shall all be lost. I feel the worm rising. It is your weight that keeps poor Death from making any progress."

I turned my head, leaning past my uncle, so as to see behind him. A long neck, surmounted by a head of indescribable horror, was slowly rising straight up out of the middle of the pool. It should not catch them! I slid down by my uncle's leg. The moment I touched the ground and let go, away went Death, and in an instant was out of sight. I was not afraid. My heart was lifted up with the thought that I was going to die for my uncle and old Death. The red worm was on the bank. It was crawling toward me. I went to meet it. It sprang from the ground, threw itself upon me, and twisted itself about me. It was a human embrace, the embrace of some one unknown that loved me!

I awoke and left the dream. But the dream never left me.

CHAPTER 26

The Evil Draws Nigher

I ROSE early, and went to my uncle's room. He was awake, but complained of headache. I took him a cup of tea, and at his request left him.

About noon Martha brought me a letter where I sat alone in the drawing-room. I carried it to my uncle. He took it with a trembling hand, read it, and fell back with his eyes closed. I ran for brandy.

"Don't be frightened, little one," he called after me. "I don't want anything."

"Won't you tell me what is the matter, uncle?" I said, returning. "Is it necessary I should be kept ignorant?"

"Not at all, my little one."

"Don't you think, uncle," I dared to continue, forgetting in my love all difference of years, "that, whatever it be that troubles us, it must be better those who love us should know it? Is there some good in a secret after all?"

prove what I say; and as to my silence for so many years, I am able thoroughly to account for it. I shall give you no further warning. You know where my son is: if he is not in my house within two days, I shall have you arrested. *I have made up my mind.*

"Lucretia Cairnedge.

"Rising-Manor, July 15, 18—."

"Whoever be the father, she's the mother of lies!" I exclaimed.—"My uncle—the best and gentlest of men, a murderer!"

I laughed aloud in my indignation and wrath.

But, though the woman was a liar, she must have something to say with a show of truth! How else would she dare intimidation with such a man? How else could her threat have so wrought upon my uncle? What did she know, or imagine she knew? What could be the something on which she founded her lie?—That my uncle was going to tell me, nor did I dread hearing his story. No revelation would lower him in my eyes! Of that I was confident. But I little thought how long it would be before it came, or what a terrible tale it would prove.

I ran down the stair with the vile paper in my hand.

"The wicked woman!" I cried. "If she *be* John's mother, I don't care: she's a devil and a liar!"

"Hush, hush, little one!" said my uncle, with a smile in which the sadness seemed to intensify the sweetness; "you do not *know* anything against her! You do not *know* she is a liar!"

"There are things, uncle, one knows without knowing!"

"What if I said she told no lie?"

"I should say she was a liar although she told no lie. My uncle is not what she threatens to say he is!"

"But men have repented, and grown so different you would not know them: how can you tell it has not been so with me? I may have been a bad man once, and grown better!"

"I know you are trying to prepare me for what you think will be a shock, uncle!" I answered; "but I want no preparing. Out with your worst! I defy you!"

Ah me, confident! But I had not to repent of my confidence!

My uncle gave a great sigh. He looked as if there was nothing for him now but tell all. Evidently he shrank from the task.

He put his hand over his eyes, and said slowly,—

"You belong to a world, little one, of which you know next to nothing. More than Satan have fallen as lightning from heaven!"

He lay silent so long that I was constrained to speak again.

"Well, uncle dear," I said, "are you not going to tell me?"

"I cannot," he answered.

There was absolute silence for, I should think, about twenty minutes. I could not and would not urge him to speak. What right had I to rouse a killing effort! He was not bound to tell *me* anything! But I mourned the impossibility of doing my best for him, poor as that best might be.

"Do not think, my darling," he said at last, and laid his hand on my head as I knelt beside him, "that I have the least difficulty in trusting you; it is only in telling you. I

would trust you with my eternal soul. You can see well
enough there is something terrible to tell, for would I
not otherwise laugh to scorn the threat of that bad
woman? No one on the earth has so little right to say
what she knows of me. Yet I do share a secret with her
which feels as if it would burst my heart. I wish it would.
That would open the one way out of all my trouble.
Believe me, little one, if any ever needed God, I need
him. I need the pardon that goes hand in hand with
righteous judgment, the pardon of him who alone can
make lawful excuse."

"May God be your judge, uncle, and neither man nor
woman!"

"I do not think *you* would altogether condemn me,
little one, much as I loathe myself—terribly as I deserve
condemnation."

"Condemn you, uncle! I want to know all, just to show
you that nothing can make the least difference. If you
were as bad as that bad woman says, you should find
there was one of your own blood who knew what love
meant. But I know you are good, uncle, whatever you
may have done."

"Little one, you comfort me," sighed my uncle. "I
cannot tell you this thing, for when I had told it, I should
want to kill myself more than ever. But neither can I bear
that you should not know it. I will *not* have a secret with
that woman! I have always intended to tell you everything. I have the whole fearful story set down for your
eyes—and those of any you may wish to see it: I cannot
speak the words into your ears. The paper I will give you
now; but you will not open it until I give you leave."

"Certainly not, uncle."

"If I should die before you have read it, I permit and desire you to read it. I know your loyalty so well, that I believe you would not look at it even after my death, if I had not given you permission. There are those who treat the dead as if they had no more rights of any kind. 'Get away to Hades,' they say; 'you are nothing now.' But you will not behave so to your uncle, little one! When the time comes for you to read my story, remember that I *now*, in preparation for the knowledge that will give you, ask you to pardon me *then* for all the pain it will cause you and your husband—John being that husband. I have tried to do my best for you, Orbie: how much better I might have done had I had a clear conscience, God only knows. It may be that I was the tenderer uncle that I could not be a better one."

He hid his face in his hands, and burst into a tempest of weeping.

It was terrible to see the man to whom I had all my life looked with a reverence that prepared me for knowing the great father, weeping like a bitterly repentant and self-abhorrent child. It seemed sacrilege to be present. I felt as if my eyes, only for seeing him thus, deserved the ravens to pick them out.

I could not contain myself. I rose and threw my arms about him, got close to him as a child to her mother, and, as soon as the passion of my love would let me, sobbed out,

"Uncle! darling uncle! I love you more than ever! I did not know before that I could love so much! I could *kill* that woman with my own hands! I wish I had killed her when I pulled her down that day! It is right to kill poison-ous creatures: she is worse than any snake!"

He smiled a sad little smile, and shook his head. Then first I seemed to understand a little. A dull flash went through me.

I stood up, drew back, and gazed at him. My eyes fixed themselves on his. I stared into them. He had ceased to weep, and lay regarding me with calm response.

"You don't mean, uncle,——?"

"Yes, little one, I do. That woman was the cause of the action for which she threatens to denounce me as a murderer. I do not say she intended to bring it about; but none the less was she the consciously wicked and wilful cause of it.—And you will marry her son, and be her daughter!" he added, with a groan as of one in unutterable despair.

I sprang back from him. My very proximity was a pollution to him while he believed such a thing of me!

"Never, uncle, never!" I cried. "How can you think so ill of one who loves you as I do! I will denounce *her!* She will be hanged, and we shall be at peace!"

"And John?" said my uncle.

"John must look after himself!" I answered fiercely. "Because he chooses to have such a mother, am I to bring her a hair's-breadth nearer to my uncle! Not for any man that ever was born! John must discard his mother, or he and I are as we were! A mother! she is a hyena, a shark, a monster! Uncle, she is a *devil!*—I don't care! It is true; and what is true is the right thing to say. I will go to her, and tell her to her face what she is!"

I turned and made for the door. My heart felt as big as the biggest man's.

"If she kill you, little one," said my uncle quietly, "I shall be left with nobody to take care of me!"

I burst into fresh tears. I saw that I was a fool, and could do nothing.

"Poor John!—To have such a mother!" I sobbed. Then in a rage of rebellion I cried, "I don't believe she *is* his mother! Is it possible now, uncle—does it stand to reason, that such a pestilence of a woman should ever have borne such a child as my John? I don't, I can't, I won't believe it!"

"I am afraid there are mysteries in the world quite as hard to explain!" replied my uncle. "I confess, if I had known who was his mother, I should have been far from ready to yield my consent to your engagement."

"What does it matter?" I said. "Of course I shall not marry him!"

"Not marry him, child!" returned my uncle. "What are you thinking of? Is the poor fellow to suffer for, as well as by the sins of his mother?"

"If you think, uncle, that I will bring you into any kind of relation with that horrible woman, if the worst of it were only that you would have to see her once because she was my husband's mother, you are mistaken. She to threaten you if you did not send back her son, as if John were a horse you had stolen! You have been the angel of God about me all the days of my life, but even to please you, I cannot consent to despise myself. Besides, you know what she threatens!"

"She shall not hurt me. I will take care of myself for your sakes. Your life shall not be clouded by scandal about your uncle."

"How are you to prevent it, uncle dear? Fulfil her threat or not, she would be sure to talk!"

"When she sees it can serve no purpose, she will hardly risk reprisals."

"She will certainly not risk them when she finds we have said good-bye."

"But how would that serve me, little one? What! would you heap on your uncle's conscience, already overburdened, the misery of keeping two lovely lovers apart? I will tell you what I have resolved upon. I will have no more secrets from you, Orba. Oh, how I thank you, dearest, for not casting me off!"

Again I threw myself on my knees by his bed.

"Uncle," I cried, my heart ready to break with the effort to show itself, "if I did not now love you more than ever, I should deserve to be cast out, and trodden under foot!—What do you think of doing?"

"I shall leave the country, not to return while the woman lives."

"I'm ready, uncle," I said, springing to my feet; "—at least I shall be in a few minutes!"

"But hear me out, little one," he rejoined, with a smile of genuine pleasure; "you don't know half my plan yet. How am I to live abroad, if my property go to rack and ruin? Listen, and don't say anything till I have done; I have no time to lose; I must get up at once.—As soon as I am on board at Dover for Paris, you and John must get yourselves married the first possible moment, and settle down here—to make the best of the farm you can, and send me what you can spare. I shall not want much, and John will have his own soon. I know you will be good to Martha!"

"John may take the farm if he will. It would be immeasurably better than living with his mother. For me, I am going with my uncle. Why, uncle, I should be miserable in John's very arms and you out of the country for our sakes! Is there to be nobody in the world but husbands, forsooth! I should love John ever so much more away with you and my duty, than if I had him with me, and you a wanderer. How happy I shall be, thinking of John, and taking care of you!"

He let me run on. When I stopped at length—

"In any case," he said with a smile, "we cannot do much till I am dressed!"

CHAPTER 2 7

An Encounter

I LEFT my uncle's room, and went to my own, to make what preparation I could for going abroad with him. I got out my biggest box, and put in all my best things, and all the trifles I thought I could not do without. Then, as there was room, I put in things I could do without, which yet would be useful. Still there was room; the content would shake about on the continent! So I began to put in things I should like to have, but which were neither necessary nor useful. Before I had got these in, the box was more than full, and some of them had to be taken out again. In choosing which were to go and which to be left, I lost time; but I did not know anything about the trains, and expected to be ready before my uncle, who would call me when he thought fit.

My thoughts also hindered my hands. Very likely I should never marry John; I would not heed that; he would be mine all the same! but to promise that I would not marry him, because it suited such a mother's plans to marry him to some one else—that I would not do to save my life! I would have done it to save my uncle's, but our exile would render it unnecessary!

At last I was ready, and went to find my uncle, reproaching myself that I had been so long away from him. Besides, I ought to have been helping him to pack, for neither he nor his arm was quite strong yet. With a heartful of apology, I sought his room. He was not there. Neither was he in the study. I went all over the house, and then to the stable; but he was nowhere, neither had anyone seen him. And Death was gone too!

The truth burst upon me: I was to see him no more while that terrible woman lived! No one was to know whither he had gone! He had given himself for my happiness! Vain intention! I should never be happy! To be in Paradise without him, would not be to be in Heaven!

John was in London; I could do nothing! I threw myself on my uncle's bed, and lay lost in despair! Even if John were with me, and we found him, what could we do? I knew it now as impossible for him to separate us that he might be unmolested, as it was for us to accept the sacrifice of his life that we might be happy. I knew that John's way would be to leave everything and go with me and my uncle, only we could not live upon nothing— least of all in a strange land! Martha, to be sure, could manage well enough with the bailiff, but John could not burden my uncle, and could not lay his hands on his own! In the mean time my uncle was gone we knew not whither! I was like one lost on the dark mountains.—If only John would come to take part in my despair!

With a sudden agony, I reproached myself that I had made no attempt to overtake my uncle. It was true I did not know, for nobody could tell me, in what direction he had gone; but Zoe's instinct might have sufficed where mine was useless! Zoe might have followed and found Thanatos! It was hopeless now!

But I could no longer be still. I got Zoe, and fled to the moor. All the rest of the day I rode hither and thither, nor saw a single soul on its wide expanse. The very life seemed to have gone out of it. When most we take comfort in loneliness, it is because there is some one behind it.

The sun was set and the twilight deepening toward night when I turned to ride home. I had eaten nothing since breakfast, and though not hungry, was thoroughly tired. Through the great dark hush, where was no sound of water, though here and there, like lurking live thing, it lay about me, I rode slowly back. My fasting and the dusk made everything in turn take a shape that was not its own. I seemed to be haunted by things unknown. I have sometimes thought whether the spirits that love solitary places, may not delight in appropriating, for embodiment momentary and partial, such a present shape as may happen to fit one of their passing moods; whether it is always the *mere* gnarled, crone-like hawthorn, or misshapen rock, that, between the wanderer and the pale sky, suddenly appals him with the sense of *another*. The hawthorn, the rock, the dead pine, is indeed there, but is it alone there?

Some such thought was, I remember, in my mind, when, about halfway from home, I grew aware of something a little way in front that rose between me and a dark

part of the sky. It seemed a figure on a huge horse. My
first thought, very naturally, was of my uncle; the next,
of the great gray horse and his rider that John and I had
both seen on the moor. I confess to a little awe at the
thought of the latter; but I am somehow made so as to
be capable of awe without terror, and of the latter I felt
nothing. The composite figure drew nearer: it was a
woman on horseback. Immediately I recalled the adventure of my childhood; and then remembered that John
had said his mother always rode the biggest horse she
could find: could that shape, towering in the half-dark
before me, be indeed my deadly enemy—she who, my
uncle had warned me, would kill me if she had the
chance? A fear far other than ghostly invaded me, and for
a moment I hesitated whether to ride on, or turn and
make for some covert, until she should have passed from
between me and my home. I hope it was something better than pride that made me hold on my way. If the
wicked, I thought, flee when no man pursueth, it ill
becomes the righteous to flee before the wicked. By this
time it was all but dark night, and I had a vague hope of
passing unquestioned: there had been a good deal of
rain, and we were in a very marshy part of the heath, so
that I did not care to leave the track. But, just ere we met,
the lady turned her great animal right across the way,
and there made him stand.

"Ah," thought I, "what could Zoe do in a race with that
terrible horse!"

He seemed made of the darkness, and rose like the
figurehead of a frigate above a yacht.

"Show me the way to Rising," said his rider.

The hard bell-voice was unmistakable.

"When you come where the track forks," I began. She interrupted me.

"How can I distinguish in the dark?" she returned angrily. "Go on before, and show me the way."

Now I had good reason for thinking she knew the way perfectly well; and still better reason for declining to go on in front of her.

"You must excuse me," I said, "for it is time I were at home; but if you will turn and ride on in front of me, I will show you a better, though rather longer way to Rising."

"Go on, or I will ride you down," she cried, turning her horse's head toward me, and making her whip hiss through the air.

The sound of it so startled Zoe, that she sprang aside, and was off the road a few yards before I could pull her up. Then I saw the woman urging her horse to follow. I knew the danger she was in, and, though tempted to be silent, called to her with a loud warning.

"Mind what you are doing, Lady Cairnedge!" I cried. "The ground here will not carry the weight of a horse like yours."

But as I spoke he gave in, and sprang across the ditch at the way-side. There, however, he stood.

"You think to escape me," she answered, in a low, yet clear voice, with a cat-like growl in it. "You make a mistake!"

"Your ladyship will make a worse mistake if you follow me here," I replied.

Her only rejoinder was a cut with her whip to her horse, which had stood motionless since taking his unwilling jump. I spoke to Zoe; she bounded off like a fawn. I pulled her up, and looked back.

Lady Cairnedge continued urging her horse. I heard
and saw her whipping him furiously. She had lost her
temper.

I warned her once more, but she persisted.

"Then you must take the consequences!" I said; and
Zoe and I made for the road, but at a point nearer home.

Had she not been in a passion, she would have seen
that her better way was to return to the road, and inter-
cept us; but her anger blinded her both to that and to the
danger of the spot she was in.

We had not gone far when we heard behind us the soft
plunging and sucking of the big hoofs through the boggy
ground. I looked over my shoulder. There was the huge
bulk, like Wordsworth's peak, towering betwixt us and
the stars!

"Go, Zoe!" I shrieked.

She bounded away. The next moment, a cry came
from the horse behind us, and I heard the woman say
"Good God!" I stopped, and peered through the dark.
I saw something, but it was no higher above the ground
than myself. Terror seized me. I turned and rode back.

"My stupid animal has bogged himself!" said Lady
Cairnedge quietly.

Deep in the dark watery peat, as thick as porridge, her
horse gave a fruitless plunge or two, and sank lower.

"For God's sake," I cried, "get off! your weight is
sinking the poor animal! You will smother him!"

"It will serve him right," she said venomously, and
gave the helpless creature a cut across the ears.

"You will go down with him, if you do not make
haste," I insisted.

Another moment and she stood erect on the back of the slowly sinking horse.

"Come and give me your hand," she cried.

"You want to smother me with him! I think I will not," I answered. "You can get on the solid well enough. I will ride home and bring help for your horse, poor fellow! Stay by him, talk to him, and keep him as quiet as you can. If he go on struggling, nothing will save him."

She replied with a contemptuous laugh.

I got to the road as quickly as possible, and galloped home as fast as Zoe could touch and lift. Ere I reached the stable-yard, I shouted so as to bring out all the men. When I told them a lady had her horse fast in the bog, they bustled and coiled ropes, put collars and chains on four draught-horses, lighted several lanterns, and set out with me. I knew the spot perfectly. No moment was lost either in getting ready, or in reaching the place.

Neither the lady nor her horse was to be seen.

A great horror wrapt me round. I felt a murderess. She might have failed to spring to the bank of the hole for lack of the hand she had asked me to reach out! Or her habit might have been entangled, so that she fell short, and went to the bottom—to be found, one day, hardly changed, by the side of her peat-embalmed steed!—no ill fitting fate for her, but a ghastly thing to have a hand in!

She might, however, be on her way to Rising on foot! I told two of the men to mount a pair of the horses, and go with me on the chance of rendering her assistance.

We took the way to Rising, and had gone about two miles, when we saw her, through the starlight, walking

steadily along the track. I rode up to her, and offered her
one of the cart-horses: I would not have trusted my Zoe
with her any more than with an American lion that lives
upon horses. She declined the proffer with quiet scorn.
I offered her one or both men to see her home, but the
way in which she refused their service, made them glad
they had not to go with her. We had no choice, therefore
turned and left her to get home as she might.

Not until we were on the way back, did it occur to me
that I had not asked Martha whether she knew anything
about my uncle's departure. She was never one to volunteer news, and, besides, would naturally think me in his
confidence!

I found she knew nothing of our expedition, as no one
had gone into the house—had only heard the horses and
voices, and wondered. I was able to tell her what had
happened; but the moment I began to question her as to
any knowledge of my uncle's intentions, my strength
gave way, and I burst into tears.

"Don't be silly, Belorba!" cried Martha, almost
severely. "You an engaged young lady, and tied so to
your uncle's apron-strings that you cry the minute he's
out of your sight! You didn't cry when Mr. Day left you!"

"No," I answered; "he was going only for a day or
two!"

"And for how many is your uncle gone?"

"That is what I want to know. He means to be away a
long time, I fear."

"Then it's nothing but your fancy sets you crying!—
But I'll just see!" she returned. "I shall know by the
money he left for the housekeeping! Only I won't budge
till I see you eat."

Faint for want of food, I had no appetite. But I began at once to eat, and she left me to fetch the money he had given her as he went.

She came back with a pocket-book, opened it, and looked into it. Then she looked at me. Her expression was of unmistakable dismay. I took the pocket-book from her hand: it was full of notes!

I learned afterward, that it was his habit to have money in the house, in readiness for some possible sudden need of it.

CHAPTER 28

Another Vision

THAT same night, within an hour, to my unspeakable relief, John came home—at least he came to me, who he always said was his home. It was rather late, but we went out to the wilderness, where I had a good cry on his shoulder; after which I felt better, and hope began to show signs of life in me. I never asked him how he had got on in London, but told him all that had happened since he went. It was worse than painful to tell him about his mother's letter, and what my uncle told me in consequence of it, also my personal adventure with her so lately; but I felt I must hide nothing. If a man's mother is a devil, it well he should know it.

He sat like a sleeping hurricane while I spoke, saying never a word. When I had ended,—

"Is that all?" he asked.

"It is all, John: is it not enough?" I answered.

"It is enough," he cried, with an oath that frightened me, and started to his feet. The hurricane was awake.

I threw my arms round him.

"Where are you going?" I said.

"To *her*," he answered.

"What for?"

"To *kill* her," he said—then threw himself on the ground, and lay motionless at my feet.

I kept silence. I thought with myself he was fighting the nature his mother had given him.

He lay still for about two minutes, then quietly rose.

"Good night, dearest!" he said; "—no; good-bye! It is not fit the son of such a mother should marry any honest woman."

"I beg your pardon, John!" I returned; "I hope *I* may have a word in the matter! If I choose to marry you, what right have you to draw back? Let us leave alone the thing that has to be, and remember that my uncle must not be denounced as a murderer! Something must be done. That he is beyond personal danger for the present is something; but is he to be the talk of the country?"

"No harm shall come to him," said John. "If I don't throttle the tigress, I'll muzzle her. I know how to deal with her. She has learned at least, that what her stupid son says, he does! I shall make her understand that, on her slightest movement to disgrace your uncle, I will marry you right off, come what may; and if she goes on, I shall get myself summoned for the defence, that, if I can say nothing for *him*, I may say something against *her*. Besides, I will tell her that, when my time comes, if I find anything amiss with her accounts, I will give her no quarter.—But, Orbie," he continued, "as I will not threaten

what I may not be able to perform, you must promise not
to prevent me from carrying it out."

"I promise," I said, "that, if it be necessary for your
truth, I will marry you at once. I only hope she may not
already have taken steps!"

"Her two days are not yet expired. I shall present
myself in good time.—But I wonder you are not afraid
to trust yourself alone with the son of such a mother!"

"To be what I know you, John," I answered, "and the
son of that woman, shows a good angel was not far off
at your birth. But why talk of angels? Whoever was your
mother, God is your father!"

He made no reply beyond a loving pressure of my
hand. Then he asked me whether I could lend him something to ride home upon. I told him there was an old
horse the bailiff rode sometimes; I was very sorry he
could not have Zoe: she had been out all day and was too
tired! He said Zoe was much too precious for a hulking
fellow like him to ride, but he would be glad of the old
horse.

I went to the stable with him, and saw him mount.
What a determined look there was on his face! He
seemed quite a middle-aged man.

I have now to tell how he fared on the moor as he rode.

It had turned gusty and rather cold, and was still a dark
night. The moon would be up by and by however, and
giving light enough, he thought, before he came to the
spot where his way parted company with that to Dumbleton. The moon, however, did not see fit to rise so soon
as John expected her: he was not at that time quite *up* in
moons, any more than in the paths across that moor.

Now as he had not an idea where his rider wanted to

be carried, and as John did for a while—he confessed it
—fall into a reverie or something worse, old Sturdy had
to choose for himself where to go, and took a path he had
often had to take some years before; nor did John discover that he was out of the way, until he felt him going
steep down, and thought of Sleipner bearing Hermod to
the realm of Hela. But he let him keep on, wishing to
know, as he said, what the old fellow was up to. Presently,
he came to a dead halt.

John had not the least notion where they were, but I
knew the spot the moment he began to describe it. By the
removal of the peat on the side of a slope, the skeleton
of the hill had been a little exposed, and had for a good
many years been blasted for building-stones. Nothing
was going on in the quarry at present. Above, it was
rather a dangerous place; there was a legend of man and
horse having fallen into it, and both being killed. John
had never seen or heard of it.

When his horse stopped, he became aware of an indefinite sensation which inclined him to await the expected moon before attempting either to advance or
return. He thought afterward it might have been some
feeling of the stone about him, but at the time he took
the place for an abrupt natural dip of the surface of the
moor, in the bottom of which might be a pool. Sturdy
stood as still as if he had been part of the quarry, stood
as if never of himself would he move again.

The light slowly grew, or rather, the darkness slowly
thinned. All at once John became aware that, some yards
away from him, there was something whitish. A moment,
and it began to move like a flitting mist through the
darkness. The same instant Sturdy began to pull his feet

from the ground, and move after the mist, which rose and rose until it came for a second or two between John and the sky: it was a big white horse, with my uncle on his back: Death and he, John concluded, were out on one of their dark wanderings! His impulse, of course, was to follow them. But, as they went up the steep way, Sturdy came down on his old knees, and John got off his back to let him recover himself the easier. When they reached the level, where the moon, showing a blunt horn above the horizon, made it possible to see a little, the white horse and his rider had disappeared—in some shadow, or behind some knoll, I fancy; and John, having not the least notion in what part of the moor he was, or in which direction he ought to go, threw the reins on the horse's neck. Sturdy brought him back almost to his stable, before he knew where he was. Then he turned into the road, for he had had enough of the moor, and took the long way home.

Mother and Son

IN the morning he breakfasted alone. A son with a different sort of mother might then have sought her in her bedroom; but John had never within his memory seen his mother in her bedroom, and after what he had heard the night before, could hardly be inclined to go there to her now. Within half an hour, however, a message was brought him, requesting his presence in her ladyship's dressing-room.

He went with his teeth set.

"Whose horse is that in the stable, John?" she said, the moment their eyes met.

"Mr. Whichcote's, madam," answered John: *mother* he could not say.

"You intend to keep up your late relations with those persons?"

"I do."

"You mean to marry the hussy?"

"I mean to marry the lady to whom you give that epithet. There are those who think it not quite safe for you to call other people names!"

She rose and came at him as if she would strike him. John stood motionless. Except a woman had a knife in her hand, he said, he would not even avoid a blow from her. "A woman can't hurt you much; she can only break your heart!" he said. "My mother would not know a heart when she had broken it!" he added.

He stood and looked at her.

She turned away, and sat down again. I think she felt the term of her power at hand.

"The man told you then, that, if you did not return immediately, I would get him into trouble?"

"He has told me nothing. I have not seen him for some days. I have been to London."

"You should have contrived your story better: you contradict yourself."

"I am not aware that I do."

"You have the man's horse!"

"His horse is in my stable; he is not himself at home."

"Fled from justice! It shall not avail him!"

"It may avail you though, madam! It is sometimes prudent to let well alone. May I not suggest that a hostile attempt on your part, might lead to awkward revelations?"

"Ah, where could the seed of slander find fitter soil than the heart of a son with whom the prayer of his mother is powerless!"

To all appearance she had thoroughly regained her composure, and looked at him with a quite artistic reproach.

"The prayer of a mother that never prayed in her life!" returned John; "—of a woman that never had an anxiety but for herself!—I don't believe you are my mother. If I was born of you, there must have been some juggling with my soul in antenatal regions! I disown you!" cried John with indignation that grew as he gave it issue.

Her face turned ashy white; but whether it was from conscience or fear, or only with rage, who could tell!

She was silent for a moment. Then again recovering herself,—

"And what, pray, would you make of me?" she said coolly. "Your slave?"

"I would have you an honest woman! I would die for that!—Oh, mother! mother!" he cried bitterly.

"That being apparently impossible, what else does my dutiful son demand of his mother?"

"That she should leave me unmolested in my choice of a wife. It does not seem to me an unreasonable demand!"

"Nor does it seem to me an unreasonable reply, that any mother would object to her son's marrying a girl whose father she could throw into a felon's-prison with a word!"

"That the girl does not happen to be the daughter of the gentleman you mean, signifies nothing: I am very willing she should pass for such. But take care. He is ready to meet whatever you have to say. He is not gone for his own sake, but to be out of the way of our happiness—to prevent you from blasting us with a public scandal. If you proceed in your purpose, we shall marry at once, and make your scheme futile."

"How are you to live, pray?"

"Madam, that is my business," answered John.

"Are you aware of the penalty on your marrying without my consent?" pursued his mother.

"I am not. I do not believe there is any such penalty."

"You dare me?"

"I do."

"Marry, then, and take the consequences."

"If there were any, you would not thus warn me of them."

"John Day, you are no gentleman!"

"I shall not ask your definition of a gentleman, madam."

"Your father was a clown!"

"If my father were present, he would show himself a gentleman by making you no answer. If you say a word more against him, I will leave the room."

"I tell you your father was a clown and a fool—like yourself!"

John turned and went to the stable, had old Sturdy saddled, and came to me.

On his way over the heath, he spent an hour trying to find the place where he had been the night before, but without success. I presume that Sturdy, with his nose in that direction, preferred his stall, and did not choose to find the quarry. As often as John left him to himself, he went homeward. When John turned his head in another direction, he would set out in that direction, but gradually work round for the farm.

John told me all I have just set down, and then we talked.

"I have already begun to learn farming," I said.

"You are the right sort, Orbie!" returned John. "I shall be glad to teach you anything I know."

"If you will show me how a farmer keeps his books," I answered, "that I may understand the bailiff's, I shall be greatly obliged to you. As to the dairy, and poultry-yard, and that kind of thing, Martha can teach me as well as any."

"I'll do my best," said John.

"Come along then, and have a talk with Simmons! I feel as if I could bear anything after what you saw last night. My uncle is not far off! He is somewhere about with the rest of the angels!"

CHAPTER 30

Once More, and Yet Again

From that hour I set myself to look after my uncle's affairs. It was the only way to endure his absence. Working for him, thinking what he would like, trying to carry it out, referring every perplexity to him and imagining his answer, he grew so much dearer to me, that his absence was filled with hope. My heart being in it, I had soon learned enough of the management to perceive where, in more than one quarter, improvement, generally in the way of saving, was possible: I do not mean by any lowering of wages; my uncle would have conned me small thanks for such improvement as that! Neither was it long before I began to delight in the feeling that I was in partnership with the powers of life; that I had to do with the operation and government and preservation of things created; that I was doing a work to which I was set by the Highest; that I was at least a floor-sweeper in the house of God, a servant for the good of his world. Existence had grown fuller and richer; I had come, like a toad out of a rock, into a larger, therefore truer universe, in which I had work to do that was wanted. Had I not been thus expanded and strengthened, how should I have patiently waited while hearing nothing of my uncle!

It was not many days before John began to press me to let my uncle have his way: where was the good any longer, he said, in our not being married? But I could not endure the thought of being married without my uncle: it would not seem real marriage without his giving me to my husband. And when John was convinced that I could not be prevailed upon, I found him think the more of me because of my resolve, and my persistency in it. For John was always reasonable, and that is more than can be said of most men. Some, indeed, who are reasonable enough with men, are often unreasonable with women. If in course of time the management of affairs be taken from men and given to women—which may God for our sakes forbid—it will be because men have made it necessary by their arrogance. But when they have been kept down long enough to learn that they are not the lords of creation one bit more than the weakest woman, I hope they will be allowed to take the lead again, lest women should become what men were, and go strutting in their importance. Only the true man knows the true woman; only the true woman knows the true man: the difficulty between men and women comes all from the prevailing selfishness, that is, untruth, of both. Who, while such is their character, would be judge or divider between them, save one of their own kind? When such ceases to be their character, they will call for no umpire.

John lived in his own house with his mother, but they did not meet. His mother managed his affairs, to whose advantage I need hardly say; and John helped me to manage my uncle's, to the advantage of all concerned. Every morning he came to see me, and every night rode back to his worse than dreary home. At my earnest request, he had a strong bolt put on his bedroom-door, the use of which he promised me never to neglect. At my suggestion too, he let it be known that he had always a brace of loaded pistols within his reach, and showed himself well practiced in shooting with them. I feared much for John.

After I no longer only believed, but knew the bailiff trustworthy, and had got some few points in his management bettered, I ceased giving so much attention to details, and allowed myself more time to read and walk and ride with John. I laid myself out to make up to him, as much as ever I could, for the miserable lack of any home-life. At Rising he had not the least sense of comfort or even security. He could never tell what his mother might not be plotting against him. He had a very strong close box made for Leander, and always locked him up in it at night, never allowing one of the men there to touch him. The horse had all the attention any master could desire, when, having locked his box behind him, he brought him over to us in the morning.

One lovely, cold day, in the month of March, with ice on some of the pools, and the wind blowing from the north, I mounted Zoe to meet John midway on the moor, and had gone about two-thirds of the distance, when I saw him, as I thought, a long way to my right, and concluded he had not expected me so soon, and had gone exploring. I turned aside therefore to join him; but had gone only a few yards when, from some shift in a shadow, or some change in his position with regard to the light, I saw that the horse was not John's; it was a gray, or rather, a white horse. Could the rider be my uncle? Even at that distance I almost thought I recognized him. It must indeed have been he John saw at the quarry! He was not gone abroad! He had been all this long time lingering about the place, lest ill should befall us! "Just like him!" said my heart, as I gave Zoe the rein, and she sprang off at her best speed. But after riding some distance, I lost sight of the horseman, whoever he was, and then saw that, if I did not turn at once, I should not keep my appointment with John. Of course had I *believed* it was my uncle, I should have followed and followed; and the incident would not have been worth mentioning, for gray horses are not so uncommon that there might not be one upon the heath at any moment, but for something more I saw the same night.

It was bright moonlight. I had taken down a curtain of my window to mend, and the moon shone in so that I could not sleep. My thoughts were all with my uncle— wondering what he was about; whether he was very dull; whether he wanted me much; whether he was going about Paris, or haunting the moor that stretched far into the distance from where I lay. Perhaps at that moment he was out there in the moonlight, would be there alone, in the cold, wide night, while I slept! The thought made me feel lonely myself: one is indeed apt to feel lonely when sleepless; and as the moon was having a night of it, or rather making a day of it, all alone with herself, why should we not keep each other a little company? I rose,

drew the other curtain of my window aside, and looked
out.

I have said that the house lay on the slope of a hollow:
from whichever window of it you glanced, you saw the
line of your private horizon either close to you, or but a
little way off. If you wanted an outlook, you must climb;
and then you were on the moor.

From my window I could see the more distant edge of
the hollow: looking thitherward, I saw against the sky the
shape of a man on horseback. Not for a moment could
I doubt it was my uncle. The figure was plainly his. My
heart seemed to stand still with awe, or was it with intensity of gladness? Perhaps every night he was thus near
me while I slept—a heavenly sentinel patrolling the
house—the visible one of a whole camp unseen, of
horses of fire and chariots of fire. So entrancing was the
notion, that I stood there a little child, a mere incarnate
love, the tears running down my cheeks for very bliss.

But presently my mood changed: what had befallen
him? When first I saw him, horse and man were standing
still, and I noted nothing strange, blinded perhaps by the
tears of my gladness. But presently they moved on, keeping so to the horizon-line that it was plain my uncle's
object was to have the house full in view; and as thus they
skirted the edge of heaven, oh, how changed he seemed!
His tall figure hung bent over the pommel, his neck
dropped heavily. And the horse was so thin that I seemed
to see, almost to feel his bones. Poor Thanatos! he
looked tired to death, and I fancied his bent knees quiv-
ering, each short slow step he took. Ah, how unlike the
happy old horse that had been! I thought of Death returning home weary from the slaughter of many kings,

and cast the thought away. I thought of Death returning home on the eve of the great dawn, worn with his age-long work, pleased that at last it was over, and no more need of him: I kept that thought. Along the sky-line they held their slow way, toilsome through weakness, the rider with weary swing in the saddle, the horse with long gray neck hanging low to his hoofs, as if picking his path with purblind eyes. When his rider should collapse and fall from his back, not a step further would he take, but stand there till he fell to pieces!

Fancy gave way to reality. I woke up, called myself hard names, and hurried on a few of my clothes. My blessed uncle out in the night and weary to dissolution, and I at a window, contemplating him like a picture! I was an evil, heartless brute!

By the time I had my shoes on, and went again to the window, he had passed out of its range. I ran to one on the stair that looked at right angles to mine: he had not yet come within its field. I stood and waited. Presently he appeared, crawling along, a gray mounted ghost, in the light that so strangely befits lovers wandering in the May of hope, and the wasted spectre no less, whose imagination of the past reveals him to the eyes of men. For an instant I almost wished him dead and at rest; the next I was out of the house—then up on the moor, looking eagerly this way and that, poised on the swift feet of love, ready to spring to his bosom. How I longed to lead him to his own warm bed, and watch by him as he slept, while the great father kept watch over every heart in his universe. I gazed and gazed, but nowhere could I see the death-jaded horseman.

I bounded down the hill, through the wilderness and

the dark alleys, and hurried to the stable. Trembling with
haste I led Zoe out, sprang on her bare back, and darted
off to scout the moor. Not a man or a horse or a live thing
was to be seen in any direction! Once more I all but
concluded I had looked on an apparition. Was my uncle
dead? Had he come back thus to let me know? And was
he now gone home indeed? Cold and disappointed, I
returned to bed, full of the conviction that I had seen my
uncle, but whether in the body or out of the body, I could
not tell.

When John came, the notion of my having been out
alone on the moor in the middle of the night, did not
please him. He would have me promise not again, for any
vision or apparition whatever, to leave the house without
his company. But he could not persuade me. He asked
what I would have done, if, having overtaken the horseman, I had found neither my uncle nor Death. I told him
I would have given Zoe the use of her heels, when *that*
horse would soon have seen the last of her. At the same
time, he was inclined to believe with me, that I had seen
my uncle. His intended proximity would account, he
said, for his making no arrangement to hear from me;
and if he continued to haunt the moor in such fashion,
we could not fail to encounter him before long. In the
meantime he thought it well to show no sign of suspecting his neighbourhood.

That I had seen my uncle, John was for a moment
convinced when, the very next day, having gone to Wittenage, he saw Thanatos carrying Dr. Southwell, my
uncle's friend. On the other hand, Thanatos looked very
much alive, and in lovely condition! The doctor would
not confess to knowing anything about my uncle, and

expressed wonder that he had not yet returned, but said he did not mind how long he had the loan of such a horse.

Things went on as before for a while.

John began again to press me to marry him. I think it was mainly, I am sure it was in part, that I might never again ride the midnight moor—"like a witch out on her own mischievous hook," as he had once said. He knew that, if I caught sight of anything like my uncle anywhere, John or no John, I would go after it.

There was another good reason, however, besides the absence of my uncle, for our not marrying: John was not yet of legal age, and who could tell what might not lurk in his mother's threat! Who could tell what such a woman might not have prevailed on her husband to set down in his will! I was ready enough to marry a poor man, but I was not ready to let my lover become a poor man by marrying me a few months sooner. Were we not happy enough, seeing each other everyday, and mostly all day long? No doubt people talked, but why not let them talk? The mind of the many is not the mind of God! As to society, John called it an oyster of a divinity. He argued, however, that probably my uncle was keeping close until he saw us married. I answered that, if we were married, his mother would only be the more eager to have her revenge on us all, and my uncle the more careful of himself for our sakes. Anyhow, I said, I would not consent to be happier than we were, until we found him. The greater happiness I would receive only from his hand.

CHAPTER 31

My Uncle Comes Home

TIME went on, and it was now the depth of a cold, miserable winter. I remember the day to which I have now come so well! It was a black day. There was such a thickness of snow in the air, that what light got through had a lost look. It was almost more like a London fog than an honest darkness of the atmosphere, bred in its own bounds. But while the light lasted, the snow did not fall. I went about the house doing what I could find to do, and wondering John did not come.

His horse had again fallen lame—this time through an accident which made it necessary for him to stay with the poor animal long after his usual time of starting to come to me. When he did start, it was on foot, with the short winter afternoon closing in. But he knew the moor by this time nearly as well as I did.

It was quite dark when he drew near the house, which

he generally entered through the wilderness and the garden. The snow had begun at last, and was coming down
in deliberate earnest. It would lie feet deep over the
moor before the morning! He was thinking what a dreary
tramp home it would be by the road—for the wind was
threatening to wake, and in a snow-wind the moor was
a place to be avoided—when he struck his foot against
something soft, in the path his own feet had worn to the
wilderness, and fell over it. A groan followed, and John
rose with the miserable feeling of having hurt some creature. Dropping on his knees to discover what it was, he
found a man almost covered with snow, and nearly insen-
sible. He swept the snow off him, contrived to get him
on his back, and brought him round to the door, for the
fence would have been awkward to cross with him. Just
as I began to be really uneasy at his prolonged absence,
there he was, with a man on his back apparently lifeless!

I did not stop to stare or question, but made haste to
help him. His burden was slipping sideways, so we lowered it on a chair, and then carried it between us into the
kitchen, I holding the legs. The moment a ray of light fell
upon the face, I saw it was my uncle.

I just saved myself from a scream. My heart stopped,
then bumped as if it would break through. I turned sick
and cold. We laid him on the sofa, but I still held on to the
legs; I was half unconscious. Martha set me on a chair, and
in a moment or two I came to myself, and was able to help
her. She said never a word, but was quite collected, looking every now and then in the face of her cousin with a
doglike devotion, but never stopping an instant to gaze.
We got him some brandy first, then some hot milk, and
then some soup. He took a little of everything we offered

him. We did not ask him a single question, but, the moment he revived, carried him up the stair, and laid him in bed. Once he cast his eyes about, and gave a sigh as of relief to find himself in his own room then went off into a light doze, which, broken with starts and half-wakings, lasted until next day about noon. Either John or Martha or I was by his bedside all the time, so that he should not wake without seeing one of us near him.

But the sad thing was, that, when he did wake, he did not seem to come to himself. He never spoke, but just lay and looked out of his eyes, if indeed it was more than his eyes that looked, if indeed *he* looked out of them at all!

"He has overdone his strength!" we said to each other. "He has not been taking care of himself!—And then to have lain perhaps hours in the snow! It's a wonder he's alive!"

"He's nothing but skin and bone!" said Martha. "It will take weeks to get him up again!—And just look at his clothes! How ever did he come nigh such! They're fit only for a beggar! They must have knocked him down and stripped him!—Look at his poor boots!" she said pitifully, taking up one of them, and stroking it with her hand. "He'll never recover it!"

"He will," I said. "Here are three of us to give him of our life! He'll soon be himself again, now that we have him!"

But my heart was like to break at the sad sight. I cannot put in words what I felt.

"He would get well much quicker," said John, "if only we could tell him we were married!"

"It will do just as well to invite him to the wedding," I answered.

"I do hope he will give you away," said Martha.

"He will never give me away," I returned; "but he will give me to John. And I will not have the wedding until he is able to do that."

"You are right," said John. "And we mustn't ask him anything, or even refer to anything, till he wants to hear."

Days went and came, and still he did not seem to know quite where he was; if he did know, he seemed so content with knowing it, that he did not want to know anything more in heaven or earth. We grew very anxious about him. He did not heed a word that Dr. Southwell said. His mind seemed as exhausted as his body. The doctor justified John's resolve, saying he must not be troubled with questions, or the least attempt to rouse his memory.

John was now almost constantly with us. One day I asked him whether his mother took any notice of his being now so seldom home at night. He answered she did not; and, but for being up to her ways, he would imagine she knew nothing at all about his doings.

"What does she do herself all day long?" I asked.

"Goes over her books, I imagine," he answered. "She knows the hour is at hand when she must render account of her stewardship, and I suppose she is getting ready to meet it;—how, I would rather not conjecture. She gives me no trouble now, and I have no wish to trouble her."

"Have you no hope of ever being on filial terms with her again?" I said.

"There can be few things more unlikely," he replied.

I was a little troubled, notwithstanding my knowledge of her and my feeling toward her, that he should regard a complete alienation from his mother with such indifference. I could not, however, balance the account between them! If she had a strong claim in the sole fact that she was his mother, how much had she not injured him simply by not being lovable! Love unpaid is the worst possible debt; and to make it impossible to pay it, is the worst of wrongs.

But, oh, what a heart-oppression it was, that my uncle had returned so different! We were glad to have him, but how gladly would we not have let him go again to restore him to himself, even were it never more to rest our eyes upon him in this world! Dearly as I loved John, it seemed as if nothing could make me happy while my uncle remained as he was. It was a kind of cold despair to know him such impassable miles from me. I could not get near him! I went about all day with a sense—not merely of loss, but of a loss that gnawed at me with a sickening pain. He never spoke. He never said *little one* to me now! he never looked in my eyes as if he loved me! He was very gentle, never complained, never even frowned, but lay there with a dead question in his eyes. We feared his mind was utterly gone.

By degrees his health returned, but apparently neither his memory, nor his interest in life. Yet he had a far-away look in his eyes, as if he remembered something, and started and turned at every opening of the door, as if he expected something. He took to wandering about the yard and the stable and the cow-house; would gaze for an hour at some animal in its stall; would watch the men threshing the corn, or twisting straw-ropes. When Dr. Southwell sent back his horse, it was in great hope that the sight of Death would wake him up; that he would recognize his old companion, jump on his back, and be well again; but my uncle only looked at him with a faint admiration, went round him and examined him as if he were a horse he thought of buying, then turned away and left him. Death was troubled at his treatment of him. He on his part showed him all the old attention, using every equine blandishment he knew; but having met with no response, he too turned slowly away, and walked to his stable. Dr. Southwell would gladly have bought him, but neither John nor I would hear of parting with him: he was almost a portion of his master! My uncle might come to himself any moment: how could we look him in the face if Death was gone from us! Besides, we loved the horse for his own sake as well as my uncle's, and John would be but too glad to ride him!

My uncle would wander over the house, up and down, but seemed to prefer the little drawing-room: I made it my special business to keep a good fire there. He never went to the study; never opened the door in the chimney-corner. He very seldom spoke, and seldomer to me than to any other. It *was* a dreary time! Our very souls had longed for him back, and thus he came to us!

Sorely I wept over the change that had passed upon the good man. He must have received some terrible shock! It was just as if his mother, John said, had got hold of him, and put a knife in his heart! It was well, however, that he was not wandering about the heath, exposed to the elements! and there was yet time for many a good thing to come! Where one *must* wait, one *can* wait.

John had to learn this, for, say what he would, the idea of marrying while my uncle remained in such plight, was to me unendurable.

CHAPTER 32

Twice Two Is One

THE spring came, but brought little change in the condition of my uncle. In the month of May, Dr. Southwell advised our taking him abroad. When we proposed it to him, he passed his hand wearily over his forehead, as if he felt something wrong there, and gave us no reply. We made our preparations, and when the day arrived, he did not object to go.

We were an odd party: John and I, bachelor and spinster; my uncle, a silent, moody man, who did whatever we asked him; and the still, open-eyed Martha Moon, who, I sometimes think, understood more about it all than any of us. I could talk a little French, John a good deal of German. When we got to Paris, we found my uncle considerably at home there. When he cared to speak, he spoke like a native, and was never at a loss for word or phrase.

It was he, indeed, who took us to a quiet little hotel he knew; and when we were comfortably settled in it, he began to take the lead in all our plans. By degrees he assumed the care and guidance of the whole party; and so well did he carry out what he had silently, perhaps almost unconsciously undertaken, that we conceived the greatest hopes of the result to himself. A mind might lie quiescent so long as it was ministered to, and hedged from cares and duties, but wake up when something was required of it! No one would have thought anything amiss with my uncle, that heard him giving his orders for the day, or acting cicerone to the little company—there for his sake, though he did not know it. How often John and I looked at each other, and how glad were our hearts! My uncle was fast coming to himself! It was like watching the dead grow alive.

One day he proposed taking a carriage and a good pair of horses, and driving to Versailles to see the palace. We agreed, and all went well. I had not, in my wildest dreams, imagined a place so grand and beautiful. We wandered about it for hours, and were just tired enough to begin thinking with pleasure of the start homeward, when we found ourselves in a very long, straight corridor. I was walking alone, a little ahead of the rest; my uncle was coming along next, but a good way behind me; a few paces behind my uncle, came John with Martha, to whom he was more scrupulously attentive than to myself.

In front of me was a door, dividing the corridor in two, apparently filled with plain plate-glass, to break the draught without obscuring the effect of the great length of the corridor, which stretched away as far on the other side as we had come on this. I paused and stood aside, leaning against the wall to wait for my uncle, and gazing listlessly out of a window opposite me. But as my uncle came nearer to open the door for us, I happened to cast my eyes again upon it, and saw, as it seemed, my uncle coming in the opposite direction; whence I concluded of course, that I had made a mistake, and that what I had taken for a clear plate of glass, was a mirror, reflecting the corridor behind me. I looked back at my uncle with a little anxiety. My reader may remember that, when he came to fetch me from Rising, the day after I was lost on the moor, encountering a mirror at unawares, he started and nearly fell: from this occurrence, and from the absence of mirrors about the house, I had imagined in his life some painful story connected with a mirror.

Once again I saw him start, and then stand like stone. Almost immediately a marvellous light overspread his countenance, and with a cry he bounded forward. I looked again at the mirror, and there I saw the self-same light-irradiated countenance coming straight, as was natural, to meet that of which it was the reflection. Then all at once the solid foundations of fact seemed to melt into vaporous dream, for as I saw the two figures come together, the one in the mirror, the other in the world, and was starting forward to prevent my uncle from shattering the mirror and wounding himself, the figures fell into each other's arms, and I heard two voices weeping and sobbing, as the substance and the shadow embraced.

Two men had for a moment been deceived like myself: neither glass nor mirror was there—only the frame from which a swing-door had been removed. They walked each into the arms of the other, whom they had at first each taken for himself.

They paused in their weeping, held each other at arm's-length, and gazed as in mute appeal for yet better assurance; then, smiling like two suns from opposing rain-clouds, fell again each on the other's neck, and wept anew. Neither had killed the other! Neither had lost the other! The world had been a graveyard; it was a paradise!

We stood aside in reverence. Martha Moon's eyes glowed, but she manifested no surprise. John and I stared in utter bewilderment. The two embraced each other, kissed and hugged and patted each other, wept and murmured and laughed, then all at once, with one great sigh between them, grew aware of witnesses. They were too happy to blush, yet indeed they could not have blushed, so red were they with the fire of heaven's own delight. Utterly unembarrassed they turned toward us— and then came a fresh astonishment, and old and new joy together out of the treasure of the divine householder: the uncle of the mirror, radiant with a joy such as I had never before beheld upon human countenance, came straight to me, cried, "Ah, little one!" took me in his arms, and embraced me with all the old tenderness. Then I knew that my own old uncle was the same as ever I had known him, the same as when I used to go to sleep in his arms.

The jubilation that followed, it is impossible for me to describe; and my husband, who approves of all I have yet written, begs me not to attempt an adumbration of it.

"It would be a pity," he says, "to end a won race with a tumble down at the post!"

CHAPTER 33

Half One Is One

I AM going to give you the whole story, but not this
moment; I want to talk a little first. I need not say that
I had twin uncles. They were but one man to the world;
to themselves only were they a veritable two. The word
twin means one of two that once were one. To *twin*
means to *divide,* they tell me. The opposite action is, of
twain to make one. To me as well as the world, I believe,
but for the close individual contact of all my life with my
uncle Edward, the two would have been but as one man.
I hardly know that I felt any richer at first for having two
uncles; it was long before I should have felt much poorer
for the loss of uncle Edmund. Uncle Edward was to me
the substance of which uncle Edmund was the shadow.
But at length I learned to love him dearly through per-
ceiving how dearly my own uncle loved him. I loved the
one because he was what he was, the other because he

was not that one. Creative Love commonly differentiates that it may unite; in the case of my uncles it seemed only to have divided that it might unite. I am hardly intelligible to myself; in my mind at least I have got into a bog of confused metaphysics, out of which it is time I scrambled. What I would say is this—that what made the world not care there should be two of them, made the earth a heaven to those two. By their not being one, they were able to love, and so were one. Like twin planets they revolved around each other, and in a common orbit around God their sun. It was a beautiful thing to see how uncle Edmund revived and expanded in the light of his brother's presence, until he grew plainly himself. He had suffered more than my own uncle, and had not had an orphan child to love and be loved by.

What a drive home that was! Paris, anywhere seemed home now! I had John and my uncles; John had me and my uncle; my uncles had each other; and I suspect, if we could have looked into Martha, we should have seen that she, through her lovely unselfishness, possessed us all more than any one of us another. Oh the outbursts of gladness on the way!—the talks!—the silences! The past fell off like an ugly veil from the true face of things; the present was sunshine; the future a rosy cloud.

When we reached our hotel, it was dinner-time, and John ordered champagne. He and I were hungry as two happy children; the brothers ate little, and scarcely drank. They were too full of each other to have room for any animal need. A strange solemnity crowned and dominated their gladness. Each was to the other a Lazarus given back from the grave. But to understand the depth of their rapture, you must know their story. That of Martha and Mary and Lazarus could not have equalled it but for the presence of the Master, for neither sisters nor brother had done each other any wrong. They looked to me like men walking in a luminous mist—a mist of unspeakable suffering radiant with a joy as unspeakable—the very stuff to fashion into glorious dreams.

When we drew round the fire, for the evenings were chilly, they laid their whole history open to us. What a tale it was! and what a telling of it! My own uncle, Edward, was the principal narrator, but was occasionally helped out by my newer uncle, Edmund. I had the story already, my reader will remember, in my uncle's writing, at home: when we returned I read it—not with the same absorption as if it had come first, but with as much interest, and certainly with the more thorough comprehension that I had listened to it before. That same written story I shall presently give, supplemented by what, necessarily, my uncle Edmund had to supply, and with some elucidation from the spoken narrative of my uncle Edward.

As the story proceeded, overcome with the horror of the revelation I foresaw, I forgot myself, and cried out—

"And that woman is John's mother!"

"Whose mother?" asked uncle Edmund, with scornful curiosity.

"John Day's," I answered.

"It cannot be!" he cried, blazing up. "Are you sure of it?"

"I have always been given so to understand," replied John for me; "but I am by no means sure of it. I have doubted it a thousand times."

"No wonder! Then we may go on! But, indeed, to believe you her son, would be to doubt you! I *don't* believe it."

"You could not help doubting me!" responded John. "—I might be true, though, even if I were her son!" he added.

"Ed," said Edmund to Edward, "let us lay our heads together!"

"Ready Ed!" said Edward to Edmund.

Thereupon they began comparing memories and recollections,—to find, however, that they had by no means data enough. One thing was clear to me—that nothing would be too bad for them to believe of her.

"She would pick out the eye of a corpse if she thought a sovereign lay behind it!" said uncle Edmund.

"To have the turning over of his rents,—" said uncle Edward, and checked himself.

"Yes—it would be just one of her devil-tricks!" agreed uncle Edmund.

"I beg your pardon, John," said uncle Edward, as if it were he that had used the phrase, and uncle Edmund nodded to John, as if he had himself made the apology.

John said nothing. His eyes looked wild with hope. He felt like one who, having been taught that he is a child of the devil, begins to know that God is his father—the one discovery worth making by son of man.

Then, at my request, they went on with their story, which I had interrupted.

When it was at length all poured out, and the last drops shaken from the memory of each, there fell a long silence, which my own uncle broke.

"When shall we start, Ed?" he said.

"To-morrow, Ed."

"This business of John's must come first, Ed!"

"It shall, Ed!"

"You know where you were born, John?"

"On my father's estate of Rubworth in Gloucester-shire, I *believe*," answered John.

"You must be prepared for the worst, you know!"

"I am prepared. As Orba told me once, God is my father, whoever my mother may be!"

"That's right. Hold by that!" said my uncles, as with one breath.

"Do you know the year you were born?" asked uncle Edmund.

"My *mother* says I was born in 1820."

"You have not seen the entry?"

"No. One does not naturally doubt such statements."

"Assuredly not—until——"

He paused.

How uncle Edmund had regained his wits! And how young the brothers looked!

"You mean," said John, "until he has known my mother!"

Now for the story of my twin uncles, mainly as written by my uncle Edward!

CHAPTER 34

The Story of My Twin Uncles

"My brother and I were marvellously like. Very few of our friends, none of them with certainty, could name either of us apart—or even together. Only two persons knew absolutely which either of us was, and those two were ourselves. Our mother certainly did not—at least without seeing one or other of our backs. Even we ourselves have each made the blunder occasionally of calling the other by the wrong name. Our indistinguishableness was the source of ever-recurring mistake, of constant amusement, of frequent bewilderment, and sometimes of annoyance in the family. I once heard my father say to a friend, that God had never made two things alike, except his twins. We two enjoyed the fun of it so much, that we did our best to increase the confusions resulting from our resemblance. We did not lie, but we dodged and pretended, questioned and looked mysterious, till I verily believe the person concerned, having in himself so vague an idea of our individuality, not unfrequently forgot which he had blamed, or which he had wanted, and became hopelessly muddled.

"A man might well have started the question what good could lie in the existence of a duality in which the appearance was, if not exactly, yet so nearly identical, that no one but my brother or myself could have pointed out definite differences; but it could have been started only by an outsider: my brother and I had no doubt concerning the advantage of a duality in which each was the other's double; the fact was to us a never ceasing source of delight. Each seemed to the other created such, expressly that he might love him as a special, individual property of his own. It was as if the image of Narcissus had risen bodily out of the watery mirror, to be what it had before but seemed. It was as if we had been made two, that each might love himself, and yet not be selfish.

"We were almost always together, but sometimes we got into individual scrapes, when—which will appear to some incredible—the one accused always accepted punishment without denial or subterfuge or attempt to perplex: it was all one which was the culprit, and which should be the sufferer. Nor did this indistinction work badly: that the other was just as likely to suffer as the doer of the wrong, wrought rather as a deterrent. The mode of behaviour may have had its origin in the instinctive perception of the impossibility of proving innocence; but had we, loving as we did, been capable of truthfully accusing each other, I think we should have been capable of lying also. The delight of existence lay, embodied and objective to each, in the existence of the other.

"At school we learned the same things, and only long after did any differences in taste begin to develop themselves.

"Our brother, elder by five years, who would succeed to the property, had the education my father thought would best fit him for the management of land. We twins were trained to be lawyer and doctor—I the doctor.

"We went to college together, and shared the same rooms.

"Having finished our separate courses, our father sent us to a German university: he would not have us insular!

"There we did not work hard, nor was hard work required of us. We went out a good deal in the evenings, for the students that lived at home in the town were hospitable. We seemed to be rather popular, owing probably to our singular likeness, which we found was regarded as a serious disadvantage. The reason of this opinion we never could find, flattering ourselves indeed that what it typified gave us each double the base and double the strength.

"We had all our friends in common. Every friend to one of us was a friend to both. If one met man or woman he was pleased with, he never rested until the other knew that man or woman also. Our delight in our friends must have been greater than that of other men, because of the constant sharing.

"Our all but identity of form, our inseparability, our unanimity, and our mutual devotion, were often, although we did not know it, a subject of talk in the social gatherings of the place. It was more than once or twice openly mooted—what, in the chances of life, would be likeliest to strain the bond that united us. Not a few agreed that a terrible catastrophe might almost be expected from what they considered such an unnatural relation.

"I think you must already be able to foresee from what the first difference between us would arise: discord itself was rooted in the very unison—for unison it was, not harmony—of our tastes and instincts; and will now begin to understand why it was so difficult, indeed impossible for me, not to have a secret from my little one.

"Among the persons we met in the home-circles of our fellow-students, appeared by and by an English lady—a young widow, they said, though little in her dress or carriage suggested widowhood. We met her again and again. Each thought her the most beautiful woman he had ever seen, but neither was much interested in her at first. Nor do I believe either would, of himself, ever have been. Our likings and dislikings always hitherto had gone together, and, left to themselves, would have done so always, I believe; whence it seems probable that, left to ourselves, we should also have found, when required, a common strength of abnegation. But in the present case, our feelings were not left to themselves; the lady gave the initiative, and the dividing regard was born in the one, and had time to establish itself, ere the provoking influence was brought to bear on the other.

"Within the last few years I have had a visit from an old companion of the period. I daresay you will remember the German gentleman who amused you with the funny way in which he pronounced certain words—one of the truest-hearted and truest-tongued men I have ever known: he gave me much unexpected insight into the evil affair. He had learned certain things from a sister, the knowledge of which, old as the story they concerned by that time was, chiefly moved his coming to England to find me.

"One evening, he told me, when a number of the ladies we were in the habit of meeting happened to be together without any gentleman present, the talk turned, half in a philosophical, half in a gossipy spirit, upon the consequences that might follow, should two men, bound in such strange fashion as my brother and I, fall in love with the same woman—a thing not merely possible, but to be expected. The talk, my friend said, was full of a certain speculative sort of metaphysics which, in the present state of human development, is far from healthy, both because of our incompleteness, and because we are too near to what we seem to know, to judge it aright. One lady was present—a lady by us more admired and trusted than any of the rest—who alone declared a conviction that love of no woman would ever separate us, provided the one fell in love first, and the other knew the fact before he saw the lady. For, she said, no jealousy would in that case be roused; and the relation of the brother to his brother and sister would be so close as to satisfy his heart. In a few days probably he too would fall in love, and his lady in like manner be received by his brother, when they would form a square impregnable to attack. The theory was a good one, and worthy of realization. But, alas, the Prince of the Power of the Air was already present in force, in the heart of the English widow! Young in years, but old in pride and self-confidence, she smiled at the notion of our advocate. She said that the idea of any such friendship between men was nonsense; that she knew more about men than some present could be expected to know: their love was but a matter of custom and use; the moment self took part in the play, it would burst; it was but a bubble-company! As for love proper—she meant the love between man and woman—its law was the opposite to that of friendship; its birth and continuance depended on the parties *not* getting accustomed to each other; the less they knew each other, the more they would love each other.

"Upon this followed much confused talk, during which the English lady declared nothing easier than to prove friendship, or the love of brothers, the kind of thing she had said.

"Most of the company believed the young widow but talking to show off; while not a few felt that they desired no nearer acquaintance with one whose words, whatever might be her thoughts, degraded humanity. The circle was very speedily broken into two segments, one that liked the English lady, and one that almost hated her.

"From that moment, the English widow set before her the devil-victory of alienating two hearts that loved each other—and she gained it for a time—until Death proved stronger than the Devil. People said we could not be parted: *she* would part us! She began with my brother. To tell how I know that she began with him, I should have to tell how she began with me, and that I cannot do; for, little one, I dare not let the tale of the treacheries of a bad woman toward an unsuspecting youth, enter your ears. Suffice it to say, such a woman has well studied those regions of a man's nature into which, being less divine, the devil in her can easier find entrance. There, she knows him better than he knows himself; and makes use of her knowledge, not to elevate, but to degrade him. She fills him with herself, and her animal influences. She gets into his self-consciousness beside himself, by means of his self-love. Through the ever open funnel of his self-greed, she pours in flattery. By depreciation of others, she hints admiration of himself. By the slightest motion of a finger, of an eyelid, of her person, she will pay him a homage of which first he cannot, then he will not, then he dares not doubt the truth. Not such a woman only, but almost any silly woman, may speedily make the most ordinary, and hitherto modest youth, imagine himself the peak of creation, the triumph of the Deity. No man alive is beyond the danger of imagining himself exceptional among men: if such as think well of themselves were right in so doing, truly the world were ill worth God's making! He is the wisest who has learned to 'be naught awhile!' The silly soul becomes so full of his tempter, and of himself in and through her, that he loses interest in all else, cares for nobody but her, prizes nothing but her regard, broods upon nothing but her favours, looks forward to nothing but again her presence and further favours. God is nowhere; fellow-man in the way like a buzzing fly—else no more to be regarded than a speck of dust neither upon his person nor his garment. And this terrible disintegration of life rises out of the most wonderful, mysterious, beautiful, and profound relation in humanity! Its roots go down into the very deeps of God, and out of its foliage creeps the old serpent, and the worm that never dies! Out of it steams the horror of corruption, wrapt in whose living death a man cries out that God himself can do nothing for him. It is but the natural result of his making the loveliest of God's gifts into his God, and worshipping and serving the creature more than the creator. Oh my child, it is a terrible thing to be! Except he knows God the saviour, man stands face to face with a torturing enigma, hopeless of solution!

"The woman sought and found the enemy, my false self, in the house of my life. To that she gave herself, as if she gave herself to me. Oh, how she made me love her! —if that be love which is a deification of self, the foul worship of one's own paltry being!—and that when most it seems swallowed up and lost! No, it is not love! Does love make ashamed? The memories of it may be full of pain, but can the soul ever turn from love with sick contempt? That which at length is loathed, can never have been loved!

"Of my brother she would speak as of a poor creature not for a moment to be compared with myself. How I could have believed her true when she spoke thus, knowing that in the mirror I could not have told myself from my brother, knowing also that our minds, tastes, and faculties bore as strong a resemblance as our bodies, I cannot tell, but she fooled me to a fool through the indwelling folly of my self-love. At other times, wishing to tighten the bonds of my thraldom that she might the better work her evil end, proving herself a powerful devil, she would rouse my jealousy by some sign of strong admiration of Edmund. She must have acted the same way with my brother. I saw him enslaved just as I —knew we were faring alike—knew the very thoughts as well as feelings in his heart, and instead of being consumed with sorrow, chuckled at the *knowledge* that *I* was the favoured one! I suspect now that she showed him more favour than myself, and taught him to put on the

look of the hopeless one. I fancied I caught at times a
covert flash in his eye: he knew what he knew! If so, poor
Edmund, thou hadst the worst of it every way!

"Shall I ever get her kisses off my lips, her poison out
of my brain! From my heart, her image was burned in a
moment, as utterly as if by years of hell!

"The estrangement between us was sudden; there
were degrees only in the widening of it. First came embarrassment at meeting. Then all commerce of wish,
thought, and speculation, ended. There was no more
merrymaking jugglery with identity; each was himself
only, and for himself alone. Gone was all brother-glad-
ness. We avoided each other more and more. When we
must meet, we made haste to part. Heaven was gone
from home. Each yet felt the same way toward the other,
but it was the way of repelling, not drawing. When we
passed in the street, it was with a look that said, or at least
meant—'You are my brother! I don't want you!' We
ceased even to nod to each other. Still in our separation
we could not separate. Each took a room in another part
of the town, but under the same pseudonym. Our common lodging was first deserted, then formally given up
by each. Always what one did, that did the other, though
no longer intending to act in consort with him. He could
not help it though he tried, for the other tried also, and
did the same thing. One of us might for months have
played the part of both without detection—especially if
it had been understood that we had parted company; but
I think it was never suspected, although now we were
rarely for a moment together, and still more rarely
spoke. A few weeks sufficed to bring us to the verge of
madness.

"To this day I doubt if the woman, our common disease, knew the one of us from the other. That in any part of her being there was the least approach to a genuine womanly interest in either of us, I do not believe. I am very sure she never cared for me. Preference I cannot think possible; she could not, it seems to me, have felt anything for one of us without feeling the same for both; I do not see how, with all she knew of us, we could have made two impressions upon her moral sensorium.

"It was at length the height of summer, and every one sought change of scene and air. It was time for us to go home; but I wrote to my father, and got longer leave."

"I wrote too," interposed my uncle Edmund at this point of the story, when my own uncle was telling it that evening in Paris.

"The day after the date of his answer to my letter, my father died. But Edmund and I were already on our way, by different routes, to the mountain-village whither the lady had preceded us; and having, in our infatuation, left no address, my brother never saw the letter announcing our loss, and I not for months.

"A few weeks more, and our elder brother, who had always been delicate, followed our father. This also remained for a time unknown to me. My mother had died many years before, and we had now scarce a relation in the world. Martha Moon is the nearest relative you and I have. Besides her and you, there were left therefore of the family but myself and your uncle Edmund—both absorbed in the same worthless woman.

"At the village there were two hostelries. I thought my brother would go to the better; he thought I would go to the better; so we met at the worse! I remember a sort of grin on his face when we saw each other, and have no doubt the same grin was on mine. We always did the same thing, just as of old. The next morning we set out, I need hardly say each by himself, to find the lady.

She had rented a small chalet on the banks of a swift mountain-stream, and thither, for a week or so, we went every day, often encountering. The efforts we made to avoid each other being similar and simultaneous, they oftener resulted in our meeting. When one did nothing, the other generally did nothing also, and when one schemed, the other also schemed, and similarly. Thus what had been the greatest pleasure of our peculiar relation, our mental and moral resemblance, namely, became a large factor in our mutual hate. For with self-loathing shame, and a misery that makes me curse the day I was born, I confess that for a time I hated the brother of my heart; and I have but too good ground for believing that he also hated me!"

"I did! I did!" cried uncle Edmund, when my own uncle, in his verbal narrative, mentioned his belief that his brother hated him; whereupon uncle Edward turned to me, saying—

"Is it not terrible, my little one, that out of a passion called by the same name with that which binds you and John Day, the hellish smoke of such a hate should arise! God must understand it! that is a comfort: in vain I seek to sound it. Even then I knew that I dwelt in an evil house. Amid the highest of such hopes as the woman roused in me, I scented the vapours of the pit. I was haunted by the dim shape of the coming hour when I should hate the woman that enthralled me, more than ever I had loved her. The greater sinner I am, that I yet yielded her dominion over me. I was the willing slave of

a woman who sought nothing but the consciousness of
power; who, to the indulgence of that vilest of passions,
would sacrifice the lives, the loves, the very souls of men!
She lived to separate, where Jesus died to make one!
How weak and unworthy was I to be caught in her snares!
how wicked and vile not to tear myself loose! The woman
whose touch would defile the Pharisee, is pure beside
such a woman!"

I return to his manuscript.

"The lady must have had plenty of money, and she
loved company and show; I cannot but think, therefore,
that she had her design in choosing such a solitary place:
its loveliness would subserve her intent of enthralling
thoroughly heart and soul and brain of the fools she had
in her toils. I doubt, however, if the fools were alive to
any beauty but hers, if they were not dead to the wavings
of God's garment about them. Was I ever truly aware of
the presence of those peaks that dwelt alone with their
whiteness in the desert of the sky—awfully alone—of the
world, but not with the world? I think we saw nothing
save with our bodily eyes, and very little with them; for
we were blinded by a passion fitter to wander the halls
of Eblis, than the palaces of God.

"The chalet stood in a little valley, high in the mountains, whose surface was gently undulating, with here
and there the rocks breaking through its rich-flowering
meadows. Down the middle of it ran the deep swift
stream, swift with the weight of its fullness, as well as the
steep slope of its descent. It was not more than seven or
eight feet across, but a great body of water went rushing
along its deep course. About a quarter of a mile from the
chalet, it reached the first of a series of falls of moderate

height and slope, after which it divided into a number of channels, mostly shallow, in a wide pebbly torrent-bed. These, a little lower down, reunited into a narrower and yet swifter stream—a small fierce river, which presently, at one reckless bound, shot into the air, to tumble to a valley a thousand feet below, shattered into spray as it fell.

"The chalet stood alone. The village was at no great distance, but not a house was visible from any of its windows. It had no garden. The meadow, one blaze of colour, softened by the green of the mingling grass, came up to its wooden walls, and stretched from them down to the rocky bank of the river, in many parts to the very water's-edge. The chalet stood like a yellow rock in a green sea. The meadow was the drawing-room where the lady generally received us.

"One lovely evening, I strolled out of the hostelry, and went walking up the road that led to the village of Auerbach, so named from the stream and the meadow I have described. The moon was up, and promised the loveliest night. I was in no haste, for the lady had, in our common hearing, said, she was going to pass that night with a friend, in a town some ten miles away. I dawdled along therefore, thinking only to greet the place, walk with the stream, and lie in the meadow, sacred with the shadow of her demonian presence. Quit of the restless hope of seeing her, I found myself taking some little pleasure in the things about me, and spent two hours on the way, amid the sound of rushing water, now swelling, now sinking, all the time.

"It had not crossed me to wonder where my brother might be. I banished the thought of him as often as it

intruded. Not able to help meeting, we had almost given
up avoiding each other; but when we met, our desire was
to part. I do not know that, apart, we had ever yet felt
actual hate, either to the other.

"The road led through the village. It was asleep. I
remember a gleam in just one of the houses. The moonlight seemed to have drowned all the lamps of the world.
I came to the stream, rushing cold from its far-off glacier-
mother, crossed it, and went down the bank opposite the
chalet: I had taken a fancy to see it from that side. Glitter-
ing and glancing under the moon, the wild little river
rushed joyous to its fearful fall. A short distance away, it
was even now falling—falling from off the face of the
world! This moment it was falling from my very feet into
the void—falling, falling, unupheld, down, down,
through the moonlight, to the ghastly rock-foot below!

"The chalet seemed deserted. With the same woefully
desolate look, it constantly comes back in my dreams. I
went farther down the valley. The full-rushing stream
went with me like a dog. It made no murmur, only a low
gurgle as it shot along. It seemed to draw me with it to
its last leap. As I looked at its swiftness, I thought how
hard it would be to get out of. The swiftness of it comes
to me yet in my dreams.

"I came to a familar rock, which, part of the bank
whereon I walked, rose some six or seven feet above the
meadow, just opposite a little hollow where the lady
oftenest sat. Two were on the grass together, one a lady
seated, the other a man, with his head in the lady's lap.
I gave a leap as if a bullet had gone through my heart,
then instinctively drew back behind the rock. There I
came to myself, and began to take courage. She had gone

away for the night: it could not be she! I peeped. The
man had raised his head, and was leaning on his elbow.
It was Edmund, I was certain! She stooped and kissed
him. I scrambled to the top of the rock, and sprang
across the stream, which ran below me like a flooded
millrace. Would to God I had missed the bank, and been
swept to the great fall! I was careless, and when I lighted,
I fell. Her clear mocking laugh rang through the air, and
echoed from the scoop of some still mountain. When I
rose, they were on their feet.

" 'Quite a chamois-spring!' remarked the lady with
derision.

"She saw the last moment was come. Neither of us two
spoke.

" 'I told you,' she said, 'neither of you was to trouble
me to-night: you have paid no regard to my wish for
quiet! It is time the foolery should end! I am weary of it.
A woman cannot marry a double man—or half a man
either—without at least being able to tell which is which
of the two halves!

"She ended with a toneless laugh, in which my brother
joined. She turned upon him with a pitiless mockery
which, I see now, must have left in his mind the conviction that she had been but making game of him; while I
never doubted myself the dupe. Not once had she received me as I now saw her: though the night was warm,
her deshabille was yet a somewhat prodigal unmasking
of her beauty to the moon! The conviction in each of us
was, that she and the other were laughing at him.

"We locked in a deadly struggle, with what object I
cannot tell. I do not believe either of us had an object.
It was a mere blind conflict of pointless enmity, in which

each cared but to overpower the other. Which first laid
hold, which, if either, began to drag, I have not a suspicion. The next thing I know is, we were in the water, each
in the grasp of the other, now rolling, now sweeping,
now tumbling along, in deadly embrace.

"The shock of the ice-cold water, and the sense of our
danger, brought me to myself. I let my brother go, but
he clutched me still. Down we shot together toward the
sheer descent. Already we seemed falling. The terror of
it over-mastered me. It was not the crash I feared, but the
stayless rush through the whistling emptiness. In the
agony of my despair, I pushed him from me with all my
strength, striking at him a fierce, wild, aimless blow—the
only blow struck in the wrestle. His hold relaxed. I remember nothing more."

At this point of the verbal narrative, my uncle Edmund
again spoke.

"You never struck me, Ed," he cried; "or if you did,
I was already senseless. I remember nothing of the
water."

"When I came to myself," the manuscript goes on, "I
was lying in a pebbly shoal. The moon was aloft in
heaven. I was cold to the heart, cold to the marrow of
my bones. I could move neither hand nor foot, and
thought I was dead. By slow degrees a little power
came back, and I managed at length, after much ago-
nizing effort, to get up on my feet—only to fall again.
After several such failures, I found myself capable of
dragging myself along like a serpent, and so got out of
the water, and on the next endeavour was able to stand.
I had forgotten everything; but when my eyes fell on
the darting torrent, I remembered all—not as a fact,

but as a terrible dream from which I thanked heaven I had come awake.

"But as I tottered along, I came slowly to myself, and a fearful doubt awoke. If it was a dream, where had I dreamt it? How had I come to wake where I found my-self? How had the dream turned real about me? Where was I last in my remembrance? Where was my brother? Where was the lady in the moonlight? No, it was not a dream! If my brother had not got out of the water, I was his murderer! I had struck him!—Oh, the horror of it! If only I could stop dreaming it—three times almost every night!"

Again uncle Edmund interposed—not altogether logi-cally:

"I tell you, I don't believe you struck me, Ed! And you must remember, neither of us would have got out if you hadn't!"

"You might have let me go!" said the other.

"On the way down the Degenfall, perhaps!" rejoined uncle Edmund. "—I believe it was that blow brought me to my senses, and made me get out!"

"Thank you, Ed!" said uncle Edward.

Once more I write from the manuscript.

"I said to myself he *must* have got out! It could not be that I had drowned my own brother! Such a ghastly thing could not have been permitted! It was too terrible to be possible!

"How, then, had we been living the last few months? What brothers had we been? Had we been loving one another? Had I been a neighbour to my nearest? Had I been a brother to my twin? Was not murder the natural outcome of it all? He that loveth not his brother is a murderer! If so, where the good of saving me from being in deed what I was in nature? I had cast off my brother for a treacherous woman! My very thought sickened within me.

"My soul seemed to grow luminous, and understand everything. I saw my whole behaviour as it was. The scales fell from my inward eyes, and there came a sudden, total, and absolute revulsion in my conscious self— like what takes place, I presume, at the day of judgment, when the God in every man sits in judgment upon the man. Had the gate of heaven stood wide open, neither angel with flaming sword, nor Peter with the keys to dispute my entrance, I would have turned away from it, and sought the deepest hell. I loathed the woman and myself; in my heart the sealed fountain of old affection had broken out, and flooded it.

"All the time this thinking went on, I was crawling slowly up the endless river toward the chalet, driven by a hope inconsistent with what I knew of my brother. What I felt, he, if he were alive, must be feeling also: how then could I say to myself that I should find him with her? It was the last dying hope that I had not killed him that thus fooled me. 'She will be warming him in her bosom!' I said. But at the very touch, the idea turned and presented its opposite pole. 'Good God!' I cried in my heart, 'how shall I compass his deliverance? Better he lay at the bottom of the fall, than lived to be devoured by that serpent of hell! I will go straight to the den of the monster, and demand my brother!' "

But to see the eyes of uncle Edmund at this point of the story!

"At last I approached the chalet. All was still. A handkerchief lay on the grass, white in the moonlight. I went up to it, hoping to find it my brother's. It was the lady's. I flung it from me like a filthy rag.

"What was the passion worth which in a moment could die so utterly!

"I turned to the house. I would tear him from her: he was mine, not hers!

"My wits were nigh gone. I thought the moonlight was dissolving the chalet, that the two within might escape me. I held it fast with my eyes. The moon drew back: she only possessed and filled it! No; the moon was too pure: she but shone reflected from the windows; she would not go in! *I* would go in! I was Justice! The woman was a thief! She had broken into the house of life, and was stealing!

"I stood for a moment looking up at her window. There was neither motion nor sound. Was she gone away, and my brother with her? Could she be in bed and asleep, after seeing us swept down the river to the Degenfall! Could he be with her and at rest, believing me dashed to pieces? I must be resolved! The door was not bolted; I stole up the stair to her chamber. The door of it was wide open. I entered, and stood. The moon filled the tiny room with a clear, sharp-edged, pale-yellow light. She lay asleep, lovely to look at as an angel of God. Her hair, part of it thrown across the top-rail of the little iron bed, streamed out on each side over the pillow, and in the midst of it lay her face, a radiant isle in a dark sea. I stood and gazed. Fascinated by her beauty? God forbid! I was fascinated by the awful incongruity between that face, pure as the moonlight, and the charnel-house that lay unseen behind it. She was to me, henceforth, not a woman, but a live Death. I had no sense of sacredness, such as always in the chamber even of a little girl. How should I? It was no chamber; it was a den. She was no woman, but a female monster. I stood and gazed.

"My presence was more potent than I knew. She opened her eyes—opened them straight into mine. All the colour sank away out of her face, and it stiffened to that of a corpse. With the staring eyes of one strangled, she lay as motionless as I stood. I moved not an inch, spoke not a word, drew not a step nearer, retreated not a hair's-breadth. Motion was taken from me. Was it hate that fixed my eyes on hers, and turned my limbs into marble? It certainly was not love, but neither was it hate.

"Agony had been burrowing in me like a mole; the half of what I felt I have not told you: I came to find my brother, and found only, in a sweet sleep, the woman who had just killed him. The bewilderment of it all, with my long insensibility and wet garments, had taken from me either the power of motion or of volition, I do not know which: speechless in the moonlight, I must have looked to the wretched woman both ghostly and ghastly.

"Two or three long moments she gazed with those horror-struck eyes; then a frightful shriek broke from her drawn, death-like lips. She who could sleep after turning love into hate, life into death, would have fled into hell to escape the eyes of the dead! Insensibility is not courage. Wake in the scornfullest mortal the conviction that one of the disembodied stands before him, and he will shiver like an aspen-leaf. Scream followed scream. Volition or strength, whichever it was that had left me, returned. I backed from the room, went noiseless from the house, and fled, as if she had been the ghost, and I the mortal. Would I had been the spectre for which she took me!"

Here uncle Edward again spoke.

"Small wonder she screamed, the wretch!" he cried: "that was her second dose of the horrible that night! You found the door unbolted because I had been there before you. I too entered her room, and saw her asleep as you describe. I went close to her bedside, and cried out, 'Where is my brother?' She woke, and fainted, and I left her."

"Then," said I, "when she came to herself, thinking she had had a bad dream, she rearranged her hair, and went to sleep again!"

"Just so, I daresay, little one!" answered uncle Edward.

"I had not yet begun to think what I should do, when I found myself at our little inn," the manuscript continues. "No idea of danger to myself awoke in my mind, nor was there any cause to heed such an idea, had it come. Nobody there knew the one from the other of us. Not many would know there were two of us. Any one who saw me twice, might well think he had seen us both. If my brother's body were found in the valley-stream, it was not likely to be recognized, or to be indeed recognizable. The only one who could tell what happened at the top of the fall, would hardly volunteer information. But, while I knew myself my brother's murderer, I thought no more of these sheltering facts than I did of danger. I made it no secret that my brother had gone over the fall. I went to the foot of the cataract, thence to search and inquire all down the stream, but no one had heard of any dead body being found. They told me that the poor gentleman must, before morning, have been far on his way to the Danube.

"Giving up the quest in despair, I resigned myself to a torture which has hitherto come no nearer expending itself than the consuming fire of God.

"I dared not carry home the terrible news, which must either involve me in lying, or elicit such confession as would multiply tenfold my father's anguish, and was in utter perplexity what to do, when it occurred to me that I ought to inquire after letters at the lodging where last we had lived together. Then first I learned that both my father and my elder brother, your father, little one, were dead.

"The sense of guilt had not destroyed in me the sense of duty. I did not care what became of the property, but I did care for my brother's child, and the interests of her succession.

"Your father had all his life been delicate, and had suffered not a little. When your mother died, about a year after their marriage, leaving us you, it soon grew plain to see that, while he loved you dearly, and was yet more friendly to all about him than before, his heart had given up the world. When I knew he was gone, I shed more tears over him than I had yet shed over my twin: the worm that never dies made my brain too hot to weep much for Edmund. Then first I saw that my elder brother had been a brother indeed; and that we twins had never been real to each other. I saw what nothing but self-loathing would ever have brought me to see, that my love to Edmund had not been profound: while a man is him-self shallow, how should his love be deep! I saw that we had each loved our elder brother in a truer and better fashion than we had loved each other. One of the chief active bonds between us had been fun; another, habit; and another, constitutional resemblance—not one of them strong. Underneath were bonds far stronger, but they had never come into conscious play; no strain had reached them. They were there, I say; for wherever is the poorest flower of love, it is there in virtue of the perfect root of love; and love's root must one day blossom into love's perfect rose. My chief consolation under the burden of my guilt is, that I love my brother since I killed him, far more than I loved him when we were all to each other. Had we never quarrelled, and were he alive, I should not be loving him thus!

"That we shall meet again, and live in the devotion of a far deeper love, I feel in the very heart of my soul. That it is my miserable need that has wrought in me this confidence, is no argument against the confidence. As misery alone sees miracles, so is there many a truth into which misery alone can enter. My little one, do not pity your uncle much; I have learned to lift up my heart to God. I look to him who is the saviour of men to deliver me from blood-guiltiness—to lead me into my brother's pardon, and enable me somehow to make up to him for the wrong I did him.

"Some would think I ought to give myself up to justice. But I felt and feel that I owe my brother reparation, not my country the opportunity of retribution. It cannot be demanded of me to pretermit, because of my crime, the duty more strongly required of me because of the crime. Must I not use my best endeavour to turn aside its evil consequences from others? Was I, were it even for the cleansing of my vile soul, to leave the child of my brother alone with a property exposing her to the machinations of prowling selfishness! Would it atone for the wrong of depriving her of one uncle, to take the other from her, and so leave her defenceless with a burden she could not carry? Must I take so-called justice on my self at her expense—to the oppression, darkening, and endangering of her life? Were I accused, I would tell the truth; but I would not volunteer a phantasmal atonement. What comfort would it be to my brother that I was hanged? Let the punishment God pleased come upon me, I said; as far as lay in me, I would live for my brother's child! I have lived for her.

"But I am, and have been, and shall, I trust, throughout my earthly time, and what time thereafter may be needful, always be in Purgatory. I should tremble at the thought of coming out of it a moment ere it had done its part.

"One day, after my return home, as I unpacked a portmanteau, my fingers slipped into the pocket of a waistcoat, and came upon something which, when I brought it to the light, proved a large ruby. A pang went to my heart. I looked at the waistcoat, and found it the one I had worn that terrible night: the ruby was the stone of the ring Edmund always wore. It must have been loose, and had got there in our struggle. Every now and then I am drawn to look at it. At first I saw in it only the blood; now I see the light also. The moon of hope rises higher as the sun of life approaches the horizon.

"I was never questioned about the death of my twin brother. One, of two so like, must seem enough. Our resemblance, I believe, was a bore, which the teasing use we made of it aggravated; therefore the fact that there was no longer a pair of us, could not be regarded as cause for regret, and things quickly settled down to the state in which you so long knew them. If there be one with a suspicion of the terrible truth, it is cousin Martha.

"You will not be surprised that you should never have heard of your uncle Edmund.

"I dare not ask you, my child, not to love me less; for perhaps you ought to do so. If you do, I have my consolation in the fact that my little one cannot make me love *her* less."

Thus ended the manuscript, signed with my uncle's name and address in full, and directed to me at the bottom of the last page.

CHAPTER 35

Uncle Edmund's Appendix

WHEN my uncle Edward had told his story, correspond-
ing, though more conversational in form, with that I have
now transcribed, my uncle Edmund took up his part of the
tale from the moment when he came to himself after their
fearful rush down the river. It was to this effect:

He lay on the very verge of the hideous void. How it
was that he got thus far and no farther, he never could
think. He was out of the central channel, and the water
that ran all about him and poured immediately over the
edge of the precipice, could not have sufficed to roll him
there. Finding himself on his back, and trying to turn on
his side in order to rise, his elbow found no support, and
lifting his head a little, he looked down into a moon-
pervaded abyss, where thin silvery vapours were stealing
about. One turn, and he would have been on his way,
plumb-down, to the valley below—say, rather, on his way

off the face of the world into the vast that bosoms the stars and the systems and the cloudy worlds. His very soul quivered with terror. The pang of it was so keen that it saved him from the swoon in which he might yet have dropped from the edge of the world. Not daring to rise, and unable to roll himself up the slight slope, he shifted himself sideways along the ground, inch by inch, for a few yards, then rose, and ran staggering away, as from a monster that might wake and pursue and overtake him. He doubted if he would ever have recovered the sudden shock of his awful position, of his one glance into the ghastly depth, but for the worse horror of the all-but-conviction that his brother had gone down to Hades through that terrible descent. If only he too had gone, he cried in his misery, they would now be together, with no wicked woman between their hearts! For his love too was changed into loathing. He too was at once, and entirely, and for ever freed from her fascination. The very thought of her was hateful to him.

With straight course, but wavering walk, he made his way through the moonlight to demand his brother. He too picked up the handkerchief, and dropped it with disgust.

What followed in the lady's chamber, I have already given in his own words.

When he fled from the chalet, it was with self-slaughter in his heart. But he endured in the comfort of the thought that the door of death was always open, that he might enter when he would. He sought the foot of the fall the same night; then, as one possessed of demons to the tombs, fled to the solitary places of the dark mountains.

He went through many a sore stress. Ignorant of the
death of his father and his elder brother, the dread misery of encountering them with his brother's blood on his
soul, barred his way home. He could not bear the
thought of reading in their eyes his own horror of himself. His money was soon spent, and for months he had
to endure severe hardships—of simple, wholesome
human sort. He thought afterward that, if he had had no
trouble of that kind, his brain would have yielded. He
would have surrendered himself but for the uselessness
of it, and the misery and public stare it would bring upon
his family.

Knowing German well, and contriving at length to
reach Berlin, he found employment there of various
kinds, and for a good many years managed to live as well
as he had any heart for, and spare a little for some worse
off than himself. Having no regard to his health, however, he had at length a terrible attack of brain-fever, and
but partially recovering his faculties after it, was placed
in an asylum. There he dreamed every night of his home,
came awake with the joy of the dream, and could sleep
no more for longing—not to go home—that he dared
not think of—but to look upon the place, if only once
again. The longing grew till it became intolerable. By his
talk in his sleep, the good people about him learning his
condition, gave and gathered money to send him home.
On his way, he came to himself quite, but when he
reached England, he found he dared not go near the
place of his birth. He remained therefore in London,
where he made the barest livelihood by copying legal
documents. In this way he spent a few miserable years,
and then suddenly set out to walk to the house of his

fathers. He had but five shillings in his possession when the impulse came upon him.

He reached the moor, and had fallen exhausted, when a solitary gypsy, rare phenomenon, I presume, with a divine spot awake in his heart, found him, gave him some gin, and took him to a hut he had in the wildest part of the heath. He lay helpless for a week, and then began to recover. When he was sufficiently restored, he helped his host to weave the baskets which, as soon as he had enough to make a load, he took about the country in a cart. He soon became so clever at the work as quite to earn his food and shelter, making more baskets while the gypsy was away selling the others. At home, the old horse managed to live, or rather not to die, on the moor, and, all things considered, had not a very hard life of it. On his back, uncle Edmund, ill able to walk so far—for he was anything but strong now, would sometimes go wandering in the twilight, or when the moon shone, to some spot whence he could see his old home. Occasionally he would even go round and round the house while we slept, like a ghost dreaming of ancient days.

"But," I said, interrupting his narrative, "the horseman I saw that night in the storm could not have been you, uncle; for the horse was a grand creature, rearing like the horse with Peter the Great on his back, in the corner of the map of Russia!"

"Were *you* out that terrible night?" he returned. "The lightning was enough to frighten even an older horse than the gypsy's.—I wonder how my friend is getting on! He must think me very ungrateful! But I daresay he imagines me lying fathom-deep in the bog.—You will do something for him, won't you, Ed?"

"You shall do for him yourself what you please, Ed," answered my own uncle, "and I will help you."

"But, uncle Edmund," I said, "if it was you we saw, the place you were in was a very boggy one always, and nearly a lake then!"

"I thought I should never get out!" he replied. "But for the poor horse and his owner, I should not have minded."

"How *did* you get out of it, uncle?" I persisted. "Lady Cairnedge smothered a splendid black horse not far from there. Through the darkness I heard him going down. It makes me shudder every time I think of it."

"I cannot tell you, child. I suppose my gray was such a skeleton that the bog couldn't hold him. I left it all to him, and he got himself and me too out of it somehow. It was too dark, as you know, to see anything between the flashes. I remember we were pretty deep sometimes."

He went back to London after that, and had come and gone once or twice, he said. When he came he always lodged with his gypsy friend. He had learned that his father was dead, but took the Mr. Whichcote he heard mentioned, for his elder brother, David, my father.

I asked him how it was he appeared to such purpose, and in the very nick of time, that afternoon when Lady Cairnedge had come with her servants to carry John away; for of course I knew now that our champion must have been uncle Edmund. He answered he had that very morning made up his mind to present himself at the house, and had walked there for the purpose, resolved to tell his brother all. He got in by the end of the garden, as John was in the way of doing, and had reached the little grove of firs by the house, when he saw a carriage at the door, and drew back. Hearing then the noises of attack and defence, he came to the window and looked in, heard Lady Cairnedge's shriek, saw her on the floor, and the men attempting to force an entrance at the other side of the window. Hardly knowing what he did, he rushed at them and beat them off. Then suddenly turning faint, for his heart was troublesome, he retired into the grove, and lay there helpless for a time. He recovered only to hear the carriage drive away, leaving quiet behind it.

To see that woman in the house of his fathers, was a terrible shock to him. Could it be that David had married her? He stole from his covert, and crawled across the moor to the gypsy's hut. There he was consoled by learning that the mistress of the house was a young girl, whom he rightly concluded to be the daughter of his brother David.

In making a second visit with the same intent, he had another attack of the heart, and now knew that he would have died in the snow had John not found him.

CHAPTER 36

The End of the First Volume

~~~

WE returned to England the next day. All the journey through, my uncles were continually reverting to the matter of John's parentage: the more they saw of him, the less could they believe Lady Cairnedge his mother. Through questions put to him, and inquiries afterward made, they discovered that, when he went to London, he had gone to Lady Cairnedge's lawyer, not his father's, of whom he had never heard—which accounted for his having on that occasion learned nothing of consequence to him. When we reached London, my uncle Edmund, who, having been bred a lawyer, knew how to act, went at once to examine the will left by John's father. That done, he set out for the place where John was born. The rest of us went home.

The second day after our arrival there, uncle Edmund came. He had found perfect proof, not only that Lady

Cairnedge was John's stepmother, but that she had no authority over him or his property whatever.

A long discussion took place in my uncles' study—I have to shift the apostrophe of possession—as to whether John ought to compel restitution of what she might have wrongfully spent or otherwise appropriated. She had been left an income by each of her husbands, upon either of which incomes she might have lived at ease; but they had a strong suspicion, soon entirely justified, that while spending John's money, she had been saving up far more than her own. But in the discussion, John held to it that, as she had once been the wife of his father, he would spare her so far—provided she had nowise impoverished either of the estates. He would insist only upon her immediate departure.

"Yes, little one," said my uncle, one summer evening, as he and I talked together, seated alone in the wilderness, "what we call misfortune is always the only good fortune. Few will say *yes* in response, but Truth is independent of supporters, being justified by her children.

"Until *misfortune* found us," he went on, "my brother and I had indeed loved one another, but with a love so poor that a wicked woman was able to send it to sleep. To what she might have brought us, had she had full scope, God only knows: *now* all the women in hell could not separate us!"

"And all the women in paradise would but bring you closer!" I ventured to add.

The day after our marriage, which took place within a month of our return from Paris, John went to Rising, on a visit to Lady Cairnedge of anything but ceremony, and took his uncles and myself with him.

"Will you tell her ladyship," he said to the footman, "that Mr. Day desires to see her."

The man would have shut the door in our faces, with the words, "I will see if my lady is at home;" but John was prepared for him. He put his foot between the door and the jamb, and his two hands against the door, driving it to the wall with the man behind it. There he held him till we were all in, then closed the door, and said to him, in a tone I had never heard him use till that moment,

"Let Lady Cairnedge know at once that Mr. Day desires to see her."

The man went. We walked into the white drawing-room, the same where I sat alone among the mirrors the morning after I was lost on the moor. How well I remembered it!

There we waited. The gentlemen stood, but, John insisting, I sat—my eyes fixed on the door by which we had entered. In a few minutes, however, a slight sound in another part of the room, caused me to turn them thitherward. There stood Lady Cairnedge, in a riding-habit, with a whip in her hand, staring, pale as death, at my uncles. Then, with a scornful laugh, she turned and went through a door immediately behind her, which closed instantly, and became part of the wainscot, hardly distinguishable. John darted to it. It was bolted on the outside. He sought another door, and ran hither and thither through the house to find the woman. My uncles ran after him, afraid something might befall him. I remained where I was, far from comfortable. Two or three minutes passed, and then I heard the thunder of hoofs. I ran to the window. There she was, tearing across the park at full gallop, on just such a huge black horse as she had smothered in the bog! I was the only one of us that saw her, and not one of us ever set eyes upon her again.

When we went over the house, it soon became plain to us that she had been in readiness for a sudden retreat, having prepared for it after a fashion of her own: not a single small article of value was to be discovered in it. John's great-aunt, who left him the property, died in the house, possessed of a large number of jewels, many of them of great price both in themselves and because of their antiquity: not one of them was ever found.

A report reached us long after, that Lady Cairnedge was found dead in her bed in a hotel in the Tyrol.

My uncles lived for many years on the old farm. Uncle Edmund bought a gray horse, as like uncle Edward's as he could find one, only younger. I often wondered what Death must think—to know he had his master on his back, and yet see him mounted by his side. Every day one or the other, most days both, would ride across the moor to see us. For many years Martha walked in at the door at least once every week.

My uncles took no pains, for they had no desire, to be distinguished the one from the other. Each was always ready to meet any obligation of the other. If one made an appointment, few could tell which it was, and nobody which would keep it. No one could tell, except, perhaps, one who had been present. which of them had signed any document: their two hands were absolutely indistinguishable, I do not believe either of them, after a time, always himself knew whether the name was his or his brother's. He could only be always certain it must have been written by one of them. But each indifferently was ready to honour the signature, *Ed. Whichcote.*

They died within a month of each other. Their bodies lie side by side. On their one tombstone is the inscription:

HERE LIE THE DISUSED GARMENTS OF

EDWARD AND EDMUND WHICHCOTE,

BORN FEB. 29, 1804;

DIED JUNE 30,

AND JULY 28, 1864.

THEY ARE NOT HERE; THEY ARE RISEN.

John and I are waiting.

Belorba Day.

Afterword

STORIES like *Lady of the Mansion** and *The Flight of the Shadow* are still commonly heard in parts of the Scottish Highlands. I recall once hearing, on a visit to Mac-Donald's birthplace of Huntly in Aberdeenshire, such a tale.

Seething with hot passions and youthful romance, it involved a legendary curse on anyone who went to the spot where on a wintry, moonlit night an enraged farmer had cut off the hands of his daughter's clandestine lover, who had come to her and was caught hanging by his hands outside the girl's bedroom window. The shadow of the boy's hands could be seen, according to the legend, on a full-moon, winter's night outside the window. But anyone who saw the shadow-hands was not supposed to live to tell about it.

---

*Originally published under the title *The Portent*.

Whether George MacDonald actually knew of this particular bizarre tale, I do not know. Certainly echoes of it can be found in *Lady of the Mansion* and *The Flight of the Shadow*—and in *Lilith*, in the scene at the end in "The House of Death," in which Adam severs the rebellious hand of Lilith. There is the violent wrestling window-scene (Ch. 24: "Hand to Hand") and the description of the farm-house given in *The Flight of the Shadow*, where Orbie lives with her uncle, which is not unlike the legendary one—"a wide, wild level, whose horizon was here and there broken by low hills." It is also similar to the way MacDonald's own boyhood home at Huntly, 'The Farm,'' looked. He returned to Huntly almost yearly and, while there, would gather material for another romance.

One of his most memorable trips North came during his last lecture-tour in the summer of 1891. He spent a few days at Huntly with his cousin James MacDonald, who then owned The Farm. It was a reflective visit filled for him, as he wrote to his wife, with moments of nostalgia: "I have just returned with James from the church-yard where the bodies of all my people are laid—a grassy place, and very quiet, in the middle of undulatory fields and with bare hills all about. But I see the country more beautiful than I used to see it. The air is delicious, and full of sweet odours, mostly white clover, and there is over it much sky. I get little bits of dreamy pleasure sometimes, but none without the future to set things right."

"I have been out for a few miles' drive," he wrote again to his wife a few days later: "to the old church of Ruthven, of which only the gable and belfry remain, with a beautiful old bell, looking quite new, though I think the date on it is 250 years old, with the legend in Latin 'Every kingdom against itself [shall] be laid waste.' Right at the foot of the belfry the fool of my story ["The Wow o' Rivven"] is buried, with a gravestone set up by the people of Huntly telling about him, and how he thought the bell, now above his body, always said, 'Come hame, come hame.' "

By the time George MacDonald wrote these words he was sixty-seven years old and had written over fifty books in thirty-six years. Facing the end of his literary career and searching for new material, he returned to his Northern home. He had in his mind at the time quite a different kind of story: "I have still one great poem in my mind," he wrote on January 4, 1891, to his daughter Lilia, "but it will never be written, I think, except we have a fortune left us, so that I need not write any more stories —of which I am beginning to be tired."

A few months before, in an attempt to produce his last "one great poem," MacDonald had written on March 28, 1890, in 50,000 words, hardly without paragraphs or punctuation, the first draft of *Lilith*, his visionary romance of dimensions. Turning again to the fantasy-romance, with which he had begun his career in writing *Phantastes*, he found in it the best imaginative vehicle for his poet's vision. In spite of the fact that MacDonald's visionary romance was, he felt—claims his son Greville—"a mandate direct from God," he had difficulty putting the story into a suitable form for publication. Thus while struggling with the Lilith-myth and his own visionary experience of it, he wrote *The Flight of the Shadow:* his prefatory romance to his final fantasy masterpiece.

There is much in *The Flight of the Shadow* which shows
the working of the Lilith-myth in MacDonald's imagination. The cosmic implications (how to convert evil) in
both stories of the struggle between human love and
diabolical hatred: the perverted, cruel mother, Lady
Cairnedge, who prefigures the child-hating temptress
Lilith. The limitless power of love to restore the consequences of evil actions—even to the point of overcoming
Death itself.

Of all the subjects which incited MacDonald's imaginative genius, the experience and meaning of death moved
him most. Death was—he insisted to the end—nothing
more than dreaming one's self into real life. Repeatedly
he wrote: "How real death makes things look! And how
we learn to cleave to the one shining fact in the midst of
the darkness of this world's trouble, that Jesus *did* rise
radiant!"

At the age of seventy, having lost his eldest daughter
Lilia and shortly before he published *Lilith,* MacDonald
wrote with resolution to a lifelong friend:

The shadows of the evening that precedes a lovelier morning are drawing down around us both. But our God is in the
shadow as in the shine, and all is and will be well: have we
not seen his glory in the face of Jesus? and do we not know
him a little? . . . This life is a lovely school time, but I never
was content with it. I look for better—oh, so far better! I
think we do not yet know the joy of mere existence. To exist
is to be a child of God; and to know it, to feel it, is to rejoice
evermore. May the loving father be near you and may you
know it, and be perfectly at peace all the way into the home
country, and to the palace home of the living one—the life of
our life.

Next month I shall be 70, and I am humbler a good deal than when I was 29. To be rid of self is to have the heart bare to God and to the neighbour—to *have* all life ours, and possess all things. I see in my mind's eye, the little children clambering up to sit on the throne with Jesus. My God, art thou not as good as we are capable of imagining thee? Shall we dream a better goodness than thou hast ever thought of? Be thyself, and all is well with us.*

For those readers of MacDonald's stories who find such optimism at times overbearing and hard to believe, I can offer no better reply than that which MacDonald gives at the end of *The Flight of the Shadow*—in the words of Uncle Edward: "That we shall meet again, and live in the devotion of a far deeper love, I feel in the very heart of my soul. That it is my miserable need that has wrought in me this confidence, is no argument against the confidence."

Glenn Edward Sadler
San Diego, California

---

*Unpublished letter. Permission to publish granted by the Trustees of the National Library of Scotland.